THOUGHT CATALOG BOOKS

From the Obscenely Strange Case Files of Dead Things Mikey

From the Obscenely Strange Case Files of Dead Things Mikey

VOLUME 1: The Presumptuous Subtitle

JOEL FARRELLY

Thought Catalog Books

Brooklyn, NY

THOUGHT CATALOG BOOKS

Copyright © 2016 by Joel Farrelly

All rights reserved. Published by Thought Catalog Books, a division of The Thought & Expression Co., Williamsburg, Brooklyn. Founded in 2010, Thought Catalog is a website and imprint dedicated to your ideas and stories. We publish fiction and non-fiction from emerging and established writers across all genres. For general information and submissions: manuscripts@thoughtcatalog.com.

First edition, 2016

ISBN 978-1945796227

10 9 8 7 6 5 4 3 2 1

Cover photography by © Joel Farrelly, design © KJ Parish

For Brad Richard, obviously...

"One of God's own prototypes… Too weird to live, and too rare to die."
–*Hunter S. Thompson*

———————

"And everything that I do is my first name."
–*Big Sean*

Contents

A Message from the Author

I need to say thank you to everyone who made this book possible. To my readers who were just as excited about the initial idea as I was, your enthusiasm means the world to me and I'd also like to add that you guys have impeccable taste.

The names below are all of those people who directly enabled the writing of this novel in some way, from time to money to both to bringing me fast food at 2 AM because I was on my grind and didn't want to stop...

So if you end up hating it, these are the folks you should blame:

Jorge Chao

Teresa Considine

Elisha Diamond

Matt Ellis

Mary Farrelly

Olivia Farrelly

Edward Halton

Sean Seebach

Kendra Syrdal

Alex Zulauf

Part 1

CASE FILE #0: "Dead Things Mikey vs. the Hoary Darkness"

1

The first time I met Dead Things Mikey, I knew I was going to write a book about him. Let the record show that I'm referring to our first meeting in for real life, or "actual meatspace" as it's known in more scientific circles. Of course, Mikey and I had been communicating via email and text for more than a month, and by then he already felt like an old friend.

Our initial correspondence began after Mikey discovered my *Thought Catalog* articles and sent me a message providing his phone number and asking if there was any percentage of my stories that wasn't complete bullshit. Though, in his defense, the question had been motivated by more than simple curiosity.

Mikey was hoping to purchase the Halloween attraction featured in a story I had written called *The Devil's Toy Box*. I politely explained how that would not be possible; less than a week after *TC* posted the article, the titular attraction was burned to the ground by several senior chairmen of the local parish council.

"So…you a big *Goonies* fan or just a total weirdo?" I asked in a joking tone and was pleased to hear laughter on Mikey's end.

When he was done chuckling, Mikey sighed and finally replied, "A little bit of both?"

"Fair enough."

"Believe it or not, in the decade or so I've been using that name as my professional title, you're one of maybe a handful of people who actually knew the reference."

"Oh, I believe THAT; no problem," I said. "Most people are terrible. It's like a rule somewhere."

2

Dead Things Mikey went on to explain that he had adopted the title during his many travels to amass what would eventually become "North America's most extensive private collection of paranormal memorabilia." To paint you a picture of what that's supposed to be:

Do you remember that scene in *The Conjuring* where the pedophile from *Hard Candy* showed off his room full of supposedly haunted objects?

Well, the third floor of Dead Things Mikey's place made that room look like some lonely housewife's porcelain tchotchke collection. His catalog of fucked-up mementos was so extensive that Mikey told me there were days when he felt more like a curator than a collector. I can't say that I blamed him.

The sizable loft which took up the bulk of Mikey's third floor certainly resembled a museum more than it did any home. The wide, narrowly divided space was sectioned off by an alternating series of standing shelves and expertly-lit glass displays. The latter was for housing the collection's more costly and/or fragile pieces. And it was indeed quite a collection. Some of its more notable entries were…

ARTIFACT #037: "The first Ouija board"

The wood is from a species of tree that went extinct sometime during the last Ice Age. The letters ornately carved into the board's surface are believed to be from a previously unknown variant of the Elamite alphabet. In place of where the moon and sun symbols would be located on a modern Ouija board (the top right and left corners respectively), there is what appears to be the head of a cuttlefish on one side and a triangle with an eye crudely etched inside of it on the other.

ARTIFACT #214: VHS tape containing CCTV footage of infamous school shooting

Common decency prevents me from disclosing which shooting. Plus, I'm pretty sure that's not the type of thing you're supposed to have. But it's worth noting that the events shown on the tape I saw didn't exactly jive with the narrative fed to us by the media. As they often are, the perpetrators in this case had been painted as yet another group of teenage pariahs with a grudge, acting out depictions of violence they had gleaned from horror movies and video games when the truth was that their real motivation had been something far more nefarious. I'd rather not go into detail, but let's just say that writing these demented fucks off as simply "maladjusted kids" is sort of like saying, "Hitler was a real jerk."

ARTIFACT #115: "Haunted" studio copy of The Beatles' album, *Let It Be*

There isn't much difference between this particular Quadraphonic 8-Track and the record that was eventually released to the public, save for a line in one song that the album's producer couldn't account for and Paul McCartney himself didn't remember singing. During the track "Two of Us," in place of the following lyrics…

> *You and I have memories—longer than the road*
> *that stretches on ahead.*

Instead, McCartney can clearly be heard singing…

> *My third eye sees dark things—a lone psycho will*
> *shoot John in the head.*

3

I was given the grand tour of this floor-length collection of rare spooky stuff that night when Mikey first invited me over to his house "for dinner and a show." Our overlapping obsessions had made us fast friends, and since Mikey was also a New Orleans native, his invite had seemed like little more than the natural progression of that friendship. Yes, sometimes I really am that gullible...

We may have both called New Orleans home, but Mikey lived just a bit above my own pay-grade. He owned a large Craftsman-style manor in the city's highly exclusive Garden District where even the most modest home will cost you roughly five times the annual salary of a drug-trafficking kingpin.

Of course, Mikey was a good fifteen years older than me and at that point I still didn't know what he actually did for a living, but I'll admit that I felt more than a little intimidated as I parked my '91 Cherokee in the circular driveway lined in luxury sedans and started up the stone walkway leading to the front door of his imposingly-sized home.

Mikey had left the gated entrance to his driveway open for me to pull my car in so that I wouldn't need to use the buzzer when I got there. I assumed that I hadn't alerted anyone to my presence as of yet and a nagging, self-conscious voice that I was all too familiar with started up inside my head...

You can still turn around right now. If you wanted to, right now you could turn around and run back to your car and flee this place forever and never look back and right now no one would be the wiser. No one's feelings would have to get hurt if you did it RIGHT NOW!

It was a comforting thought that was immediately doused by the large oak front door swinging open to reveal a handsome middle-aged man with the bleached-white teeth of a Disney Channel celebrity and the haircut to match. Mikey was dressed in a teal tailored blazer and black designer skinny jeans.

His shoes were matching teal Converses, which immediately caused me to ask, "Where did you get teal Converses?"

"The Internet." Mikey pointed at me as he asked, "Joel?"

I aimed a thumb over my shoulder and said in a joking tone, "No, I just thought you had a cool house and decided to pull in. Is that weird?"

Mikey laughed and I immediately felt better. I've found that if I can make someone laugh, they're usually a lot more forgiving of my...let's call them idiosyncratic tendencies.

"You ARE joking?" Mikey asked, his tone suddenly turning serious as he widened his eyes at me.

"I am," I said, nodding promptly.

Mikey exhaled in relief and replied, "Good. Also, just curious: you're not like a total homophobe, right?"

"What? NO. I went to art school..."

Mikey opened the front door wide enough for me to enter and replied, "Great. Otherwise, it was going to get really awkward when I introduced you to my husband."

4

Mikey's husband was named Mauricio and he was about my own age, though that's where our similarities ended. Mauricio had the classic good looks and toned physique of a movie star and he smelled like the mahogany-lined office of a prestigious boat captain. And contrary to what most of my nicknames in high school would lead you to believe, I'm about as straight as they come. That being said, even I thought Mauricio was a total catch.

"OH! the guy who writes those stories," he said, sounding excited when Mikey introduced us. We had just entered their predictably massive kitchen and Mauricio quickly replaced the lid on the pot he had been checking. He wiped his hands on a nearby towel before offering the right one to shake as he continued, "I was super excited to hear you were coming. Michael made me read your article…the one with the cam-girl? I REALLY liked it."

I shook Mauricio's outstretched hand, genuinely impressed by his comment. "Really? That's my strangest piece by far and THAT is saying something."

"Normally, I hate scary stuff, too, and he knows it." Mauricio waved a hand at Mikey and then turned back to check the simmering pan in front of him as he said, "When he told me what it was about, I was like, 'There's no way this guy is coming over for dinner.' But then I started reading it. I couldn't stop, which is also rare. I'm not normally a big reader but I don't know. I loved the Enid character. She reminded me so much of my sister."

I hadn't realized Mikey left the kitchen until I opened my mouth to respond and he suddenly returned, holding an old white landline office phone and abruptly derailing my train of thought as he held up the phone and said, "Check it out."

"It's...an old-ass telephone."

Mikey smirked at me and was about to reply when a gray-haired woman in horn-rimmed glasses who looked like she could've been your local librarian's older, more socially awkward sister suddenly leaned in from the hallway and said...

"Is this a bad time?"

Mikey's interest in me immediately vanished as he turned to face the woman and said, "Not if you're about to tell me what I think you are."

The old woman sighed and closed her eyes before finally answering, "She checks out."

"FUCKIN' A!" Mikey shouted so loudly that it startled the rest of us. He raised his arms in a victorious gesture and started to exit the room as I turned to give Mauricio a questioning look.

He smirked at my expression, his eyes trailing the woman as she followed Mikey out of view and then finally Mauricio said, "That's Lynn. The little old lady thing is an act. She was a cop. Detective, actually. She worked homicide for like twenty years. Now, Michael keeps her on retainer as his resident skeptic."

"So like his Scully?"

Something behind me caught Mauricio's attention and he nodded. "I think you're being summoned..."

I turned to see Mikey leaning back into the kitchen and waving me over as he said, "You're going to want to hear this."

5

I followed Mikey down a hallway lined in chic sconces and framed Egon Schiele prints. From somewhere upstairs, I could faintly hear Bob Seger singing...

Started hummin' a song from 1962. Ain't it funny how the night moves?

And that's when I finally realized where I was...

"You live in a Bret Easton Ellis novel," I said matter of factly to Mikey's back and he responded with a polite chuckle that sounded forced, and I realized that to him, I might as well have said, "I'm way poorer than you."

This realization had me feeling self conscious, which of course caused my social anxiety to flare back up just in time for us to reach a closed door located near the end of the hallway. Mikey opened the door, gesturing for me to enter. As I stepped inside the sparsely furnished interrogation-room, the sudden transition caught me off guard.

It was the first room I'd seen in the entire house that didn't look like something out of Tim Gunn's wet dream. The walls were bare and painted a faded pink that made me feel genuinely uneasy. The room's only furniture was a scarred wooden table and three chairs.

Mikey sat down at the table, gesturing for me to take the seat beside his. He set the landline phone down on the table and said, "This is why I invited you over. My newest addition to the collection..."

Dead Things Mikey gestured down at the bulky white anachronism in front of him and I took a beat before finally replying, "Okay?"

"Are you familiar with the term *provenance*?'"

I nodded. "Yeah, it's French for 'how I will sell you bullshit.'"

Mikey chuckled again, this one sounding a bit more genuine than the last. "Most of the time, you'd be right. But when you're dealing with paranormal artifacts, it's all ABOUT the provenance. And this one's a doozy."

Mikey pressed a switch on the intercom terminal that was mounted to his corner of the table. The thing looked to be circa-1981 and there was even a crackling hiss as the com went hot and Mikey said, "Grace?"

He let off the switch and a moment later, another crackle-hiss preceded a tired female voice replying, "Bring her in?"

CRACKLE-HISS... "Ten-four."

CRACKLE-HISS... "WHAT?"

CRACKLE-HISS... "Yes."

CRACKLE-HISS... "Yes, bring her in?"

CRACKLE-HISS... "YES."

I had been expecting to see the librarian/detective enter through the secondary door to our left, though I guess the completely different voice I'd heard over the intercom should've tipped me off. But that's okay, I bet the look on my face when Grace entered was fucking priceless.

This girl was the kind of beautiful that is almost irritating. Looking at her was like looking at a real-life equivalent of the uncanny valley. I could describe her but why bother? You're already picturing the version you know best. I should probably also mention that she was dressed as Janet from *Rocky*

Horror Picture Show, wearing white barely-there lingerie and matching high heels.

And that was because Grace had been participating in a local screening of *Rocky Horror* when Mikey called to ask if she would come in and lend a hand with tonight's sale. Grace was in such a rush to get here that she had forgotten to change back into her civvies before leaving the theater.

Of course, when she arrived no one had considered her outfit to be much of an issue; not even Grace who assumed she was only going to be around a couple of gay dudes, maybe Old Scully, and tonight's seller who was a woman named Janet (she had entered behind Grace but I barely noticed.)

The overly exposed beauty queen forcefully waved at me as she guided the other woman over to the chair positioned across from us. Grace's awkward gesture caught me by surprise and it took a moment to figure out why she had done it. My mouth was hanging open and I had been staring at Grace like a total creeper as she approached the table in what seemed like slow motion. I quickly blinked and looked away as I totally, for sure played it off.

"Thanks for telling me some rando was here," Grace said with a cold scowl as she turned and started toward the door.

"Sorry. I forgot you were wearing... that," Mikey replied, gesturing at the half-naked hot girl's attire. Grace let out a scoff and exited the room, slamming the door behind her as Mikey turned to me and said, "I didn't forget."

"Aw, that's not right," I said in a chastising tone. "But thank you."

Mikey held up his closed fist and we bumped knuckles. He then turned to address the woman sitting across from us as he smiled politely and said, "My apologies. This is my associate, the writer Joel Farrelly..."

Mikey's word-choice made me laugh and I added, "The ONLY one."

"I'm sorry to ask you to go through all of this again..."

Janet held up a hand and said, "PLEASE, for the money you're paying...plus, it's kind of nice just to talk about all of this with someone who doesn't think I'm, you know...bat-shit insane?"

Mikey nodded and gave her a genial smile. "Happy to help."

"And you have. More than you may ever know. My sister..." There was a very abrupt pause and then finally Janet continued, "She would've liked you."

6

Christine ("Chris" to those closest to her) wasn't just Janet's baby sister; she was also her best friend. It had been that way since their dad murdered their mom when Janet was sixteen and Chris was only twelve.

Their father had received a life sentence for his crime, and to spare the girls from having to spend the rest of their childhood in foster care, a family court judge sent them to live with their senile grandmother. This meant that at an age when she should've been spending her time gushing over whatever a One Direction is, Janet had been all but raising her younger sibling.

Though the truth was that Janet wouldn't have had it any other way (discounting a way in which her dad hadn't killed her mom, of course.) Janet loved her sister more than any other person on this earth; Chris was essentially the only real family she had left at that point. Plus, Janet always felt a bit guilty about not having been there when her mother was murdered, especially since Chris had been.

She managed to hide in a hall closet when the fighting began and just outside this closet was where their father, a military veteran and subsequent borderline schizophrenic who had been suffering from a severe bout of PTSD, ended up stabbing their mom to death.

That day took years for Chris to get over. She developed a number of social disorders as a result and experienced severe night terrors throughout her adolescence. Chris was eventually able to work past her issues and even grew up to be a confident, sociable woman.

When she first got the job at the call center, Chris thought she was going to love it but the place turned out to be a total shithole. It didn't help that most of her coworkers were way older than Chris and the manager, Jerry, was a professional-level creep. Still, the job (booking hotel rooms for people too stupid to work the Internet) wasn't all that bad with one big asterisk next to that statement in the form of the cheap desk phone she had been issued along with her cubicle.

Even though it was a landline, calls would constantly drop out on her and the phone's "hold" button often required several presses before responding. Still, none of this would've been quite so annoying if Chris hadn't been working at a CALL CENTER. When she asked a co-worker about it, Chris was informed that she had one of the newer model phones Jerry recently started issuing as replacements.

Apparently, management had been made aware of the newer obviously cheaper model's issues; he just didn't care. Luckily, Chris happened upon one of the older phones buried in the back of the supply closet while digging for printer paper later that same afternoon. The phone seemed to work just fine and after that, her job became a lot more bearable…

For about a day. The call center was a 24-hour operation and part of being the newest hire was that Chris often got scheduled to work the graveyard shift from 10 PM to 7 AM, as was the case that next night.

Things were literally business as usual for the first hour or so. The shine still hadn't quite worn off her new/old phone when Chris got a call request from an unknown number, which was weird because the system was supposed to boot those. She declined the call manually and a moment later, the phone began to ring once more. According to the display, it was another unknown number.

Chris glanced back at where the two other people on tonight's skeleton crew should have been sitting but one was on their lunch break and the other was smoking a cigarette out back. She shrugged at the empty room and accepted the call.

Chris ran through the standard greeting with an affectation that was already beginning to sound rehearsed, concluding with, "How can I be of service today?"

"There was a murder tonight at the Houston [HOTEL REDACTED], the one on Melvin Harris Boulevard." The man who said this sounded old; his voice was something just above a whisper and muffled like he was talking into his cupped hand.

"Um, well, we...I'm sorry, that's not what we..." Chris began to stutter in reply but the man quickly cut her off as he continued...

"I'm on my way to the one in Dallas right now. There's going to be a murder there, too."

At that moment, Chris's coworker returned from his smoke break and the expression on her face must have been pretty telling because he took one look at her and said, "What? What's wrong?"

Chris disconnected the call and told him what the man had said and they called Jerry, who wasn't exactly thrilled to have to come back to the office after contacting the Houston hotel and learning that the caller's claim was no joke. A woman had been stabbed to death while using the ice machine less than an hour earlier and no one had seen her killer.

The Houston police called to question Chris about her conversation with the man on the phone, and as the kids say, shit got pretty real after that. There was a coordinated effort with officers at the hotel in Dallas to prevent another murder, but of course, it didn't do any good, and about an hour after they arrived on scene, a second victim's body was discovered in an elevator.

Part of the fallout from this whole ordeal was that Chris got fired. The official reason had been "negligent job performance" and the excuse they gave her was that she was the one to accept a call from an unknown number and ultimately put the company at risk. Chris was made to clean out her desk that very same night and she ended up taking the new/old phone with her out of simple spite.

Janet received a call from her baby sister a few nights later. Chris sounded distraught, claiming that the phone she had taken from work (which was still in its cardboard box by the front door), had started to ring. It wasn't plugged into anything and Chris didn't even have a landline connection at her place.

Thinking the thing was malfunctioning, Chris took the phone out of the box and turned it over to see if she could get the case off. As she did this, the receiver fell loose from its cradle and a familiar voice began to emanate from the phone…

"In a few minutes, there's going to be a murder at your apartment complex."

Chris tossed the phone across the room and immediately

pulled out her cell to call Janet. She had just finished relaying all of this to her when there was a knock on Chris's door that was loud enough for Janet to hear it through the phone.

The sudden sound made both of them jump and Janet shouted, "Don't answer it!"

"Don't worry. I wasn't..."

Those were the last words Chris spoke to her sister, or anyone for that matter. The line went dead and police found her mutilated remains slumped in the open doorway of her apartment. The M.E. noted that Chris clearly put up a fight, though it had been no use. Of course, there were no witnesses to the crime and without a hit on the DNA or any real leads to follow up on, the case (though still technically open) was ultimately pushed aside to focus on more pressing matters.

7

"I told the cops everything Chris had told me. Of course, it didn't matter," Janet said, looking forlorn, her eyes fixed on the bare wall to her left.

As Janet concluded her story, Mikey casually placed something in my lap. I glanced down to see that it was a small fire extinguisher as Mikey laid his other hand palm up on the table in a comforting gesture and said, "In the end, you were there for her. That's what matters."

Janet turned to face him and I could see the tears welling in her eyes as she placed her hand in Mikey's and said, "Thank you. For everything…"

"Don't mention it," he replied with a wink as Mikey used his free hand to pat the top of hers and Janet suddenly caught fire. I mean like her entire body ERUPTED INTO FLAMES. It was as if her skin had been replaced with magnesium flash paper.

"The FUCK?!" I screamed, jumping to my feet and reflexively spraying Janet with the fire extinguisher I was holding as she let out a horrific shriek.

"Relax," Mikey said as the fire consuming Janet's body quickly fizzled out, revealing nothing but a charcoal husk reminiscent of the remains found at Pompeii. He motioned to the chair I had just vacated. "Sit down. I'll explain."

"Oh, you'll explain?"

"Uh-huh."

"Explain how you just made a person spontaneously fucking combust?!"

"She wasn't a person. I mean, she was at some point but just then, she was a skinwalker. What the kids today would mislabel as a zombie, though the term 'zombie' refers specifically to a LIVING person being controlled by an autonomous source. Reanimated dead are a whole 'nother thing."

Mikey nodded down at the slowly dissolving ash heap where Janet used to be and continued, "Now, normally she wouldn't have gotten past the front gate but I let this one in to illustrate a point."

"To WHO?"

"To you," Mikey said in a matter-of-fact tone that made me feel kind of dumb for not realizing it.

"If anyone cares, I thought the whole thing was unnecessarily risky and terribly stupid, but what do I know?" Lynn the Warrior Librarian said as she followed Grace back into the interrogation room. The latter was now wearing a trench coat that was way too big on her and carrying a broom.

I took another beat to let Mikey's words sink in (if you're familiar with my work, then you know why I require a considerably short adjustment period for this sort of thing.) After silently reminding myself not to stare at the obnoxiously attractive Grace as she began to sweep up Janet's ashes, I turned to face Mikey.

"And what would that point be, exactly?" I said, trying my best to sound calm.

"That if you're going to be hanging around, you'll need to learn how to spot the many human abominations one encounters in our line of work."

"Since when is 'collector of the paranormal' a line of work?"

Mikey shook his head as he smiled at Lynn and replied, "The collection upstairs is merely a hobby facilitated by my occupation."

"And what is your occupation?"

Mikey turned back to face me as he said, "Call it paranormal tech support."

I couldn't help but scoff. "You saying you're a Ghostbuster?"

"That's putting a bit too fine of a point on it for my liking. Plus, I think the title might be taken."

I pointed a hand at Mikey in a defiant gesture and replied, "Ghost Whisperer. Whatever. I still don't get what you'd need me for?"

Mikey looked almost bashful as he said, "Essentially, I need someone to transcribe the events of my job on a case-by-case basis and I'd prefer that someone be you. All I ask is that you maintain the anonymity of our clients. The going rate for the service we provide is a hefty one, and obviously with this job discretion is key. And of course, you're free to do whatever you want with the finished case files. All I ask is that you write them."

"Interesting…One last question. Actually, it's the same one as before: How did you make her burst into flames like that?"

"Ah," Mikey said with a smirk as he held up the hand he had placed over Janet's and pointed to his ring finger, revealing what looked like a small wooden shark's tooth fixed to the bottom of his wedding band. "A piece of the actual cross Jesus was crucified on. Most of the corpses you're going to find around here are hardwired to some facet of the Judeo-Christian faith. Nine out of ten times, this little baby will force the reanimated vessel into a sort of hard reboot, reducing them to ash before you can say 'walking dead guy.' Or girl, in this case."

"Right, sure…and WHY do you have dead people coming after you?"

"Currently?"

"Yes, why are the living dead infiltrating your home CURRENTLY?"

Mikey shrugged and said, "The price you pay for putting a necromancing con artist out of business."

"Okay, hashtag real talk? That DOES sound like an awesome story."

"Plus, I'll pay you. A lot. Tell him, Grace."

Grace stopped sweeping up Janet to shrug and gesture at the floor as she said, "You think I'd be here otherwise?"

I took a moment to consider this and then sighed as I finally said, "Fuck it. Why not?"

"Huzzah!" Mikey cheered, raising his arms.

8

Grace responded to his enthusiastic gesture with an amused smirk as she continued to sweep and Lynn quickly turned to examine the iPad in her hands. This had been a subtle ruse meant to conceal her eye roll, though something on the screen seemed to genuinely catch her attention.

"Why am I detecting motion in the backyard?" Lynn said as she tapped at the iPad and then showed it to Mikey. He examined the screen and was about to respond when the telephone on the table in front of us began to ring. Just a reminder; this was the same landline telephone from Janet's story. Its cord was currently coiled up beside the phone and very much NOT plugged in.

By the third ring, Mikey reached out a hand to answer it but I managed to stop him by shouting, "WHAT?!"

"What?" Mikey said, echoing my question with his hand hovering over the ringing phone.

"How is answering that NOT a terrible idea?!"

"Now I'm getting exterior breach alerts for the front and side motion detectors, as well," Lynn said to no one in particular. Mikey turned to glare at the ringing telephone.

"It's fine, I promise. It's just Linus attempting another stunt from his big bag of sad parlor tricks. It would almost be adorable at this point if he wasn't trying to murder me and everyone I love."

I set down the fire extinguisher I had been clutching and

opened the voice recorder app on my phone as I said, "Linus the NECROMANCER?"

"That one, yeah."

"Well, at least put it on speaker so we can all hear," I said, and Mikey nodded before pressing a button on the phone as I held my cell to it and hit record.

Mikey grinned and leaned in close to the phone as he said, "Hey there, Linus Infection. Bad news. It looks like you're gonna be short one meat puppet for dinner."

What we heard in response sounded like several dozen voices speaking in unison. Because of this, it was hard to decipher exactly what they were actually saying at first but after listening to the recording about a hundred times, I'm pretty sure it was…

WHEN THE HOARY DARKNESS DIED, ITS BODY WAS BURNED AND THE ASHES SCATTERED TO THE WIND. IT WAS FROM THESE ASHES THAT MAN FIRST AROSE AND THOUGH CAPABLE OF SO MANY TERRIBLE THINGS, SOMEHOW HE BECAME CONVINCED THAT WHAT PUT HIM HERE HAD DONE SO WITH GOOD INTENTIONS. *

*[Credit goes to Mikey for the "hoary" part because I thought they were saying something COMPLETELY different.]

Just as the line went dead, we heard Mauricio shout from somewhere down the hall, "Michael?! You need to come see this…"

Lynn, Grace, and I followed Mikey out of the interrogation room and then down a second hallway which led into a spacious den. The room's far wall was almost entirely comprised of a single bay window looking out onto Mikey's expansive front lawn. Through this window, we could see what looked like a thin film of black smoke crawling across the lawn and slowly but surely approaching the house.

"What the fuck IS that?" Mauricio asked Mikey as we entered the room. The smoke began to climb up the outside of the window, flattening against the glass and reducing our view to an opaque black void.

Mikey replied, "The Hoary Darkness."

Mauricio nodded at the wall of smoke. "Well, tell that bitch to get off my lawn."

A face suddenly emerged from the wall of black smoke. It was the face of a girl I was dating at the time, her eyes tightly closed and her expression one of pure agony.

"Pee-paw?" Grace muttered, a look of disbelief on her face as she began to approach the window.

"That's not your Pee-paw," Mikey said as he quickly placed a hand on her shoulder. "Okay, everybody! Panic room, now!"

9

Mauricio let out a defiant scoff as he pointed a thumb back toward the kitchen and said, "My sauce is gonna burn."

"Panic room NOW!" Mikey repeated as he glared at Mauricio, who responded by rolling his eyes and gesturing for us to follow as he said…

"Come on."

Mauricio led us back into the hallway and I realized I had left my cell phone in the interrogation room, so I ducked back in to grab it as we passed. Then I saw the old landline phone on the table and reflexively froze as I said, "Oh, shit."

"What?" Lynn asked, pausing just outside the room and glancing in at me.

She followed my gaze to the table and figured it out for herself when she saw that the phone had been split into several pieces, the top of its bulky plastic casing peeled back as if something had exploded out of it. Or more accurately, HATCHED out of it.

I nodded at the phone and said, "I'm gonna assume that's a bad sign."

"What's a bad sign?" Mikey asked.

He had been trailing behind the rest of us and sprinkling holy water in our wake while quietly chanting in what I think was Latin. He finished blessing the first section of hallway and was turning to face us when he spotted the phone for himself and froze.

For the first and only time that night, Mikey looked genuinely concerned as he muttered, "Oh, shit…"

"What does it mean?" I asked, despite honestly not wanting to know what it took to put that look on Mikey's face. Though it quickly became a moot point; he didn't get a chance to answer me before Grace's scream suddenly reverberated through the room like a shrill gunshot.

Mikey disappeared down the hallway in a flash, running toward the sound of her voice with Lynn sprinting after him. I started to follow suit when Mikey suddenly reappeared in the doorway, almost plowing into me as he reentered the interrogation room and grabbed the fire extinguisher from off of the table.

I quickly leaped aside as Mikey started back into the hall. I hurried to follow him and was just in time to glimpse what at first appeared to be a large mass of dryer lint swarming Grace. Then Mikey started spraying her with the fire extinguisher and she was enveloped in an off white fog. As the fog began to dissipate, I saw that the dryer lint was now falling off of Grace in clumps.

Mikey stomped on each new piece as it fell loose. That's when I realized the clumps of lint were actually fuzzy white spiders roughly the size of mice. Their limbs were long and thin, resembling those of an abnormally large Daddy Longlegs. If you squinted, you could just barely make out the tiny human-like head attached to the front of each one, their faces vaguely resembling that of a demonic infant and their mouths a churning mass of thin, pointy teeth.

By now, the swarm of babyface spiders had dissolved most of Grace's trench coat but had yet to actually harm her before

Mikey used the fire extinguisher to blast them loose. He yanked Grace to her feet and then snapped his head around to face me as he shouted, "Let's go!"

As I followed Mikey down the hallway to the panic room, I heard a faint clicking sound above me and looked up to see a second, much larger swarm of white spider-things scurrying across the ceiling. Just as I spotted them, one of the spiders let out a disturbingly childlike wail and dropped down toward me.

I managed to make it inside the panic room just as the little fucker started to dive-bomb my head (just thinking about it now is still enough to make me shudder.) Mikey pushed the heavy steel door shut behind me and it slid closed with a pressurized *THUNK*.

"What the hell, Mikey?!" Grace screamed.

I glanced at her and saw that the tattered remains of her trench coat were no longer doing such a great job at covering her risqué undergarment. After several seconds, I forced myself to look away (because I'm a goddamn gentleman) and turned to address Mikey.

"The girl's got a point."

Mikey nodded as he yanked open a nearby drawer and began to rummage through it. "I'll admit I hadn't anticipated such a well-coordinated attack from someone like Linus. That's my bad."

Lynn let out an indignant scoff that was part "I told you so" and part "No shit, Sherlock!"

Mikey paused his rummaging to give her a pleading look and then he continued, "But you have nothing to worry about. Everything is going to be fine. If I can survive a night at Nicolas Cage's house, I sure as hell can handle this novice level, clown shoes bullshit…ah-HA! Here we go."

Mikey retrieved a thin, ornately engraved stone pipe from the drawer and glanced inside the bowl before lighting it and taking a long drag. As Mikey exhaled a cloud of sweet-smelling smoke, he saw me staring at the apparatus in his hand and held it up.

"H.P. Lovecraft's opium pipe," he said, pointing at it.

I nodded and asked, "You think that's the best idea right now?"

Mikey shrugged as he glanced at the pipe and said, "I cleaned it first."

"And what are you smoking out of it?"

"Opium," he replied in a matter-of-fact tone. Mikey took another hit.

"It makes NO sense," Lynn nearly screamed and let out a frustrated groan. She was staring at a bank of security monitors mounted to one wall of the panic room and watching as the horde of spider-things began to make their way into the den. "The Darkness is an easy summon but why the fay spiders?"

"Because they're transcorporal," Mikey responded through another exhale of smoke. He started over to the bank of monitors and continued, "Linus knew I'd have every entrance to this place protected…"

"Do you?" Grace asked, sounding more than a little worried.

"I had eleven different holy men bless every doorway, window, and air vent. Plus, a coven of white-hat Wiccans comes by once a month to renew a barrier of protection."

"Wait, so FUCK! They're gonna..." Lynn stopped in mid sentence, her eyes widening with realization as she turned back to examine the security feed of the living room.

"They're gonna what?" I asked before I was even aware of the question leaving my mouth.

They both glanced at me and then Mikey turned back to face Lynn as he said, "Not if I can help it."

"Help WHAT?!" I shouted in frustration.

Mikey nodded at Mauricio and asked, "You remember that box of arts and crafts supplies I had you stash in here? Can you grab it?"

Mauricio nodded and nearly sprinted into a small alcove at the back of the room containing a row of large gray supply cabinets. As he was rummaging through the cabinets, Mikey turned to face me and finally began to explain...

"The mortal plane's inhabitants are divided into three tiers: corporeal, discorporeal, and transcorporeal. Because of their physiological makeup, a corporeal entity like you or I cannot physically affect a discorporeal entity. Those are ghosts, wraiths, poltergeists, what have you. But a transcorporeal being like a species of fay or 'fairy' would be able to affect both...that's fairy-like with the dust, not like Mauricio."

Mauricio paused his search to let out an exaggerated gasp and shouted in a mock offended tone, "Ex-CUSE me?!"

Mikey replied with a smirk and a wink as Grace snapped her fingers at him and chided, "Now is not the time for opium and kitschy dialog! FOCUS!"

I was pretty sure I was starting to get it and said, "They're going to dissolve your protection barrier?"

Mikey nodded and exhaled another cloud of opium smoke

as he replied, "They'll probably chew through the door, too, just to be dicks about it. Luckily, I'm not gonna let 'em get much farther than that."

Mauricio returned with a box of colored tape and other assorted supplies as Lynn narrowed her eyes at Mikey and said, "Care to share exactly how you plan on stopping them?"

Mikey glanced back at Lynn and nodded. "I'm going to become their god."

10

Mikey took one last hit from Lovecraft's pipe and then he got to work. While Lynn and Grace kept us updated on the spiders' progress, I watched Mikey assemble a crude mask that depicted (according to him) the likeness of the fay god, Lobos.

By the time Lynn informed us that the spiders had eaten through the front door and were starting to lead the Hoary Darkness down the hall to the panic room, Mikey had just finished stapling the makeshift straps into place and he slid the finished mask on.

"And how are you so sure this is going to work?" Grace asked, still sounding concerned.

"Ancient Chinese secret," Mikey said as he reached a hand inside his blazer to retrieve the crumpled remains of a dead fay spider and the rest of us responded with a chorus of disgusted groans.

Mikey continued, "While I was in the Orient a few years back, I met an old mystic who taught me a few tricks…"

Mikey snapped off one of the spider's legs and used it to coat his palms in a thin film of fay blood, which was mostly clear with a faint gold shimmer to it.

"This one is called 'the Perfect Mask,'" Mikey said.

He then pressed his hands to the mask covering his face and quietly chanted a few indecipherable words. When he pulled his hands away a moment later, we all screamed. The crude Lobos mask had suddenly been replaced by something that can only be described as the hideous and disfigured mug of a giant demon baby.

"Pretty neat, huh?" the twisted, demonic-looking infant face said to me in Mikey's voice. I slowly nodded.

"They're almost through," Lynn nearly shouted, her tone bordering on genuine fear.

Mikey turned around just in time to watch the center of the panic room's steel door buckle inward and then burst open to reveal the horde of fay spiders that began to swarm inside. They quickly dissolved the rest of the door, clearing a path for the Hoary Darkness in all its cloudy black glory.

"Hey, World's Most Obnoxious Bong Hit? Now would be a good time to start running," Mikey said as he approached the black cloud snaking its way into the room.

The same ex's face that I had seen before emerged out of the approaching darkness and the many voices talking at once started up again, asking…

WHAT FOOLISH MORTAL WOULD DARE THREATEN THE HOARY DARKNESS?

Mikey held his arms out and replied, "I'm Dead Things Mikey…and your shit is clown shoes."

As Mikey clapped his hands together, the ring of fay spiders surrounding the doorway began to swarm the Hoary Darkness and I had to cover my ears with my hands to muffle the sound of what seemed like a thousand different voices crying out in pain.

11

After the Hoary Darkness had been consumed and Lynn and Grace had finally left, Mikey made his way out to the backyard where he found me reclining beside the rocky facade of a fake waterfall feeding into his giant swimming pool. I had wanted to hang back so I could talk to Mikey one-on-one about his offer.

As he approached, Mikey said, "Wait, don't tell me. Let me guess. You'll take the job and you can't wait to start."

I forced a smile and sat up as Mikey lowered himself onto the chaise lounge beside me. I sighed and took a beat to formulate my response…

"I have some concerns."

Mikey retrieved a remote from the small glass table between us and aimed it at the pool as he thumbed a button which turned off the roaring waterfall. The backyard was suddenly a lot quieter as he said, "Like…"

"Like how I couldn't help but notice that you endangered all of our lives tonight just to prove a point."

"I can see how that might make for a poor first impression," Mikey said as he turned to gaze into his pool. "But if you're waiting for me to apologize, I have bad news. This is what we do for a living. Our job is to deal with stuff like tonight on a routine basis."

Mikey gestured at our surroundings and continued, "If you hadn't noticed, though, business is pretty good. So, yeah, we go hard around here but my people knew what they were signing up for. I make absolutely sure of that."

I thought about this and after a beat, I slowly nodded at the pack of fay spiders that had obediently followed Mikey out here as I asked, "What are you gonna do with them?"

Mikey glanced down at the horde of disgusting spiderthings and said, "Not sure yet. I was planning on organizing them into some kind of *battle royale* or something and then just flushing the last one but they've kind'a grown on me."

"I wonder what you'd have to feed them."

Mikey frowned and shook his head as he said, "Trust me. You don't wanna know."

Of course, if that were true, I wouldn't have taken the job.

Part 2

CASE FILE #1: "Dead Things Mikey and the Curious Occurrence on Humbug Hill"

1

It was just after dawn that next Saturday morning. The sound of my cell phone pulled me from a genuinely pleasant dream, which is a rarity in my field. I knew who was calling even before I looked at the screen and read the name "Dead Things Mikey" displayed above a smirking photo of my new boss.

"Good morning, Mikey."

"Thank god! You're up! I need you to come to the Wily Tower downtown. Like immediately. There's a keycard waiting for you at the front desk. If they give you any shit, just ask for Raoul."

Nobody gave me any shit but the concierge who introduced himself as Raoul still insisted on accompanying me over to the bank of classy glass elevators at the back end of the Wily's marble-floored lobby. We entered one of the elevators and Raoul hit a button labeled "P" because of course, Mikey had booked the penthouse suite.

We rode up in silence and when the elevator doors finally slid open again with an artificial chime, Raoul gestured down the hallway to the left and smiled. I tried to tip him a five-spot, but Raoul refused to take it.

"I thank you," the concierge said in a clipped, ESL tone. "But Mr. Things Mikey is a regular guest of the Wily and he takes great care in providing for us. As he would say, his friends do not have good money here."

I shrugged and gladly shoved the crumpled Lincoln back

into my pocket as I exited the elevator and turned to nod at him. "You're a good man."

"I do apologize."

"For what, being awesome? Let me tell you something, Raoul. You can't go through life worrying what other people think about you. Look at me…" I waved a hand at myself and continued, "Clearly, also awesome. Last week, I told my family and respective loved ones that I was quitting my day job so some rich gay dude could pay me to transcribe his ghost whispering. You think they were supportive about it?"

Raoul nodded and hit a button on the elevator's inside panel. "Very good, sir."

"Hell no! Those prude micks shit enough bricks to build a goddamn house but did I let that stop me? Nope! And that house would be disgusting, Raoul. Think about it…DISGUSTING. And here I am anyway because fuck what people think."

The elevator doors began to slide closed and Raoul's awkward smile finally dropped away as he looked down and sighed, muttering something in Spanish. Luckily, Mikey already had me in the habit of wearing a pen-sized microrecorder whenever I was "on the job." I had the forethought to thumb the little switch to "REC" in the elevator and according to my buddy, Christian, Raoul said…

"In Cabo, I was a surgeon. Seriously, man? You took three years of Spanish."

In case you couldn't tell, I was still feeling a bit nervous about the drastic life-altering change I'd recently made by accepting Mikey's job offer. Even after I signed the one-year contract he emailed me, it still didn't feel real. My cousin who's a lawyer looked the whole thing over beforehand and he said the terms were so good, the only possible issue would be the Feds thinking I was a professional rentboy.

I asked my cousin why that would be a bad thing and he explained what a "rentboy" was and that made me want to rewatch Midnight Cowboy, which was not the best idea under the circumstances. It's a great movie but all it did that night was bum me out.

Now here I was, Harry Nilsson's angelic voice WHA-UH-WHA-ing in my head while I gaped at my own exhausted reflection in the closed elevator doors of some swanky downtown hotel way too early on a Saturday morning and looking like a walk of shame played in reverse.

I won't let you leeeeeeeave...

I told Nilsson to cram it and turned to stare down the corridor before me, which was a good bit wider than your typical hotel hallway. It was lined in a gaudy patterned carpet that was vaguely disorienting to look at for too long, an effect which naturally drew my eye to the lavish set of double doors at the other end...

Fuck you, carpet! I'll get there when I'm damn good and ready!

With a heavy sigh, I started toward the penthouse entrance. Even though Raoul had given me a keycard, I still knocked. PRO-TIP: Don't ever enter a hotel room that isn't explicitly yours without knocking first. There are things in this world that you can't unsee, like what the captain of my college debate team looked like with a dildo strapped to his forehead (the answer being "a bald, sweaty unicorn.")

From inside the penthouse, I heard Mikey shout, "Joely Poley?"

"I told you don't call me that. "

"Joelseph Poleseph?"

I slowly shook my head as I slid the keycard into its slot and pushed open the door. I entered and glanced around, half expecting to find Lil' Wayne accompanied by a drum loop and some big bootied bitches because, holy shit, you guys! Have you ever been in an upscale metropolitan hotel penthouse? And not just during your *Entourage*-themed daydreams. Like REALLY been inside one?

And if you have, don't take this the wrong way, but fuck you, dude. You're really screwing with my story here. I don't care if it was an accident. It was a dick move and you're ruining this for everyone. As for the rest of you…

Like seriously, it was awesome. I could see the Superdome from the couch in the living room! It had a living room! I didn't see Mikey at first but then I started across the seemingly vacant den and, from overhead, I heard him say, "What's up?"

I looked up to see Mikey pinned to the ceiling above me. He was completely naked and his arms were extended in either direction like Jesus, or maybe just a guy who caught a really big fish.

"Very punny." I gave the penthouse another cursory scan and asked, "Where's Mauricio?"

"In Honduras, tending to his dying mother. That's why I'm here. I can't stand being in that huge house by myself."

"Aw, is she okay?"

"His mother? She's about a hundred and a black-hearted

bitch from hell who used to treat my Cio like an ashtray. So, no. Okay is not what she is."

"Jesus. Why would he ever go back there?"

"Because his mother is dying. You mind if we worry about my thing now?"

2

I nodded and Mikey continued, "See that small nest of what look like quartz crystals on the table there?"

I spotted them and nodded again. "I do."

"They are currently generating a gravitational anomaly."

"Cool!"

"Right? There's this guy I get 'em from in Pasadena. He told me he's the Dalai Lama. Usually, anyway. The last time he died, there was a hiccup in the system and he was reborn the bastard son of a syphilitic prostitute instead. But the silver lining is that every full moon, he sheds all of his hair and excretes this molten plasma that hardens into these crystals when it cools."

I gestured at the crystals and said, "Well that makes perfect sense."

"The guy could've been lying. I mean, he was on a LOT of meth."

"So, can I just ask: Are you tucking your junk like Buffalo Bill for my benefit or because it makes you feel pretty?"

"Obviously, it's the gravitational anomaly!" Mikey sighed and continued, "And if we're being honest, a little bit of the second one. To get an effect this strong, you need to arrange the crystals just right. I had the bright idea to superglue 'em in place while I was sitting here alone getting shitty drunk, and I left it out. Woke up in the middle of the night and went to the kitchen to make a snack. It was dark and of course I tripped over the fucking coffee table..."

"So what's with the, uh, full-on dude nudity?"

"I sleep naked. I'm sorry I'm not an animal."

"Literally every animal sleeps naked."

"A fair point. Say, would you mind if we saved this debate for AFTER you get me down?"

Mikey instructed me to slide the couch into the coffee table, pushing the table aside and also providing him with a soft place to land when he abruptly fell from the ceiling a moment later. Mikey quickly stood and cupped his junk as he nodded at me. "Thank you."

"Anytime. So, was that it or..."

"Not quite. We've got a case." Mikey said as he turned and started toward the hallway. "It's a bit of a drive and we'll more than likely be spending the night there so if you want to stop off for a change of clothes on the way out, we can. Now, if you'll excuse me, I'm gonna go have myself a well-earned bowel movement and shower."

I nodded and replied, "Speaking of clothes, were you planning to wear them on this road trip?"

"I was flirting with the idea...hey, Joel!" Mikey suddenly spun around to point his finger at me as he said, "You always have nerdy video game shit on your shirts."

"Not ALWAYS...sometimes it's comic books."

"I meant it as a good thing. I was wondering if you knew how to get an old DOS game running on a newer computer."

I let out a scoff and, in what has to be the most condescending tone anyone has ever used to answer that question, I said, "I do."

"Perfect."

When Mikey had returned from his shower, I handed him a graphing calculator which was currently emitting the sounds of gunfire and grunting. Mikey began to thumb the keys as he said, "What is this? What am I doing?"

"That is id Software's 1993 classic, *Doom*, and what you are doing is playing it on a calculator. You were wondering if I knew anything about making old games run on stuff. Now you don't have to wonder."

Of course, I had my laptop and Mikey used his phone to email me the game file, which he said was his only lead in the case he was currently working. We made our way down to Mikey's Porsche and I had the game running before we were out of the hotel's parking garage. According to the title screen, it was called...

HELPLESS HERMAN AND THE HELL UNDER HUMBUG HILL

Below that were the words "a game by Jeb Casteel." Though the game itself was more or less a clone of the popular '80s title, *Boulder Dash*, only with one notable caveat: despite its graphical limitations, *Helpless Herman* had one of the most disturbing opening sequences I had ever experienced in a game.

HERMAN HAD A DAD WHO DRANK AND WAS ALWAYS MEAN SO ONE DAY HERMAN RAN AWAY TO LIVE ON HUMBUG HILL WHICH WAS HIS FAVORITE PLACE IN THE WHOLE WORLD.

HERMAN DIDN'T KNOW IT BUT THERE WAS AN OLD WELL AT THE TOP OF HUMBUG HILL THAT THE ADULTS HAD FORGOTTEN TO SEAL OFF. HERMAN FELL IN THE WELL WHICH WAS JUST BARELY WIDER THAN HIM AND NO ONE EVER CAME TO SAVE HIM HERMAN WAS HELPLESS...

Hey, Helpless Herman! I can help you, if it's help you really want. But it will cost you a million jewels to leave my maze or you will never see sunlight again!

At this point, the actual game began as the dialog box disappeared to reveal an underground labyrinth of claustrophobic dirt pathways and murderous rocks waiting to crush you at every wrong turn. We stopped at a diner for lunch and I brought my laptop inside so I could show the game to Mikey who watched me play it while chewing his food in thoughtful silence.

"Basically, you're the scary face there near the center and your objective is to collect the jewels while avoiding rocks which fall when you dig the dirt out from under them. You can also trap yourself between boulders for which there is even a suicide button, see?"

I demonstrated by tapping the S key (you moved using the arrow keys, very old-school) and another dialog box appeared below Herman which read:

Are you sure you want to die? Y/N

"If you pick yes, it says 'Too bad!' And then it restarts you at the beginning of the first stage."

"What happens if you pick no?"

"You just stay stuck where you are."

"Forever?"

"Presumably, yes."

"That's pretty dark."

We finished lunch and Mikey caught me up on his new case as we resumed our road trip.

"About ninety miles northeast of here, there's a town called Clear Lake where things seem pretty normal from a distance. The Clear Lake town council is still making its weekly updates to the municipal website and all of the local businesses are caught up on their taxes but according to reports and confirmed by Lynn and Grace who are there right now, it's been a ghost town for almost two weeks. Not a single human in site."

"You're telling me in two weeks, no one who's noticed this has contacted the authorities?"

"Of course they did. Who do you think called me? Chris Carter got it wrong. The Federal Bureau of Investigation could never get away with spending their already limited resources on something as superfluous as the X-Files."

"That argument is actually a key plot point in the series," I abruptly added, causing Mikey to roll his eyes.

"AS I was saying...you need to remember this is America. When there's a problem not covered by the skill set of public authority, the government turns to private contractors to get the job done. Even then, they'll usually find a way to make some other private corporation foot the bill."

I tilted my head at him and asked, "How do they manage that?"

"Usually, it's the corporation's fault to begin with."

I snapped my fingers and pointed at Mikey as I said, "Oh! Like when a housing developer builds suburbs over an ancient Native American burial ground and then you have to show up to stop Coach's house from imploding."

Mikey shrugged at me as he replied, "Sort of. There was the time when BP awoke that dormant Kraken under the Gulf of Mexico or in this case, where the check came from a major chemical manufacturer with a facility just outside of Clear Lake. Something like ninety percent of the facility's employees were residents of the town and the manufacturer would like to know what happened to them about as much as it would probably DISLIKE a public investigation into where they went."

"So where does Helpless Herman come in then?"

"Well, the first thing I noticed when the case came to me was a discrepancy. One of those municipal website updates I mentioned was a town census which contained a name that hadn't appeared on there since the eighties. The name of a young boy who went missing a little over thirty years ago...Jeb Casteel."

"That's the name on the game's title screen."

Mikey nodded and said, "Yesterday, Lynn was able to locate Jeb's middle school records, which contained some notes about possible parental abuse and a floppy disk with that game on it. Apparently, the kid was only twelve and already a gifted programmer when he disappeared."

I knew how "gifted" you would actually have to be to make a retitled clone of *Boulder Dash*. When I was twelve, I was making my own community maps for *Duke Nuke'Em* and I was an idiot, as evidenced by my most popular map being titled "Joel Takes His Big Dick Out and Oh My God It's So Big V_3." But I kept my mouth shut because I wasn't the type to speak ill of possibly dead children.

Instead, I simply asked, "Is there a Humbug Hill in Clear Lake?"

"Not officially. I checked. But it could be a colloquial title. Like the nickname teenagers used for a make-out spot, something of that nature. Too bad there's no one there that we can ask."

It wasn't immediately after that line when Mikey's cell started ringing, but let's pretend it was for the sake of pacing. He glanced down at the name on the screen.

"It's Lynn. Hold on." Mikey accepted the call and put the phone to his ear as he said, "Whatcha got?"

Mikey paused to listen and then turned to look at me as he replied, "Interesting…"

3

We met Lynn and Grace at a motel about 20 miles outside of Clear Lake. By the time Mikey and I arrived, the sun had almost set and we pulled into the motel's parking lot with the last strands of twilight still clinging to the horizon behind us. It gave everything a strange pink hue that was just short of unsettling.

I tried to convince myself that the salmon-colored sky was a result of the manufacturing facility located about a mile up the road and I was probably right, but the knowledge did little to settle the knot in my stomach as we drove up to the motel's front office to see Lynn and Grace waiting just inside, both women looking back at us through the glass door with identical expressions of exhausted relief. We entered the small building to greet them and I gave Grace a polite nod.

She responded by immediately turning to Mikey and saying, "So he's gonna be like a regular occurrence now? That's just fucking great."

Mikey furrowed his brow at her and started to answer but I cut him off as I replied, "Look, this whole Ross and Rachel will-they-won't-they thing we got going is no picnic on my end either, but if you could refrain from blatantly flirting with me while we're on the clock, I'd really appreciate it."

Mikey began to laugh. Grace just stood there, looking pissed and glaring at me through ice-cold murder eyes. Mikey pointed at the front desk as his laughter finally faded to a sigh and he said, "Lynn, you wanna go get us checked in? Four rooms."

"On it," Lynn replied as he handed her a credit card. Mikey then turned to Grace and gestured back at the entrance.

"You wanna take a walk to the car with me?"

"Take a WHAT?"

"We need to have a word," Mikey said as he moved to the door and held it open for Grace, whose murderous expression momentarily turned to confusion before finally landing on annoyed as she looked back at Mikey with a posture that said, *Are you fucking kidding me?*

Mikey's posture responded with, *No, I'm fucking not.*

This was all very new to me. There weren't a lot of intense exchanges of body language and dramatic rivalries with hot girls at any of my previous jobs. To be honest, the whole thing was starting to make me feel incredibly awkward.

When Grace followed Mikey outside and the door finally swung shut behind them, I let out a sigh of relief so loud that Lynn turned to look back at me as she finished checking us in. She approached a moment later with several key cards in hand and I was initially embarrassed but then I saw that Lynn's expression was one of empathetic resolve. She nodded at Grace through the glass door.

"I get it. I love the girl but she can be a bit…overly intense sometimes. She has her reasons and of course, that's probably why Mikey chose Grace to begin with. He responds to intensity."

We were watching Mikey and Grace argue through the glass door, the two of them backlit by a polluted pink sky while trading frantic gestures as I slowly nodded and said, "Tell me about it."

"And it's never easy being the new kid but there's something you need to understand, if you haven't figured it out already. Mikey is grooming both of you for the same thing."

"Yeah? What's that?"

"What do you think?" Lynn replied and then scoffed at me when all I could do was shrug. "It's only child syndrome. This is something that Grace wants very badly and for a long time, she was Mikey's only real candidate. So of course, she sees you as her competition. Right now, he's out there reminding her..."

Mikey appeared to be intently describing something to Grace as Lynn motioned at him and continued, speaking almost in sync with the movement of Mikey's lips...

"That's not how this works. We are a team and could not properly function otherwise..."

As Grace shouted something back at Mikey, Lynn said, "The truth is Mikey will groom as many potential protégés as he can find. For a gay man, he's got a very hetero obsession with leaving behind little versions of himself. And god knows that girl has enough daddy issues to fight him every step of the way. So, this should be fun."

Lynn quietly muttered that last sentence to me just before Mikey re-entered the office and asked, "We all set?"

"Yep. You are..." Lynn said, examining the four key card sleeves in her hand. "Room nine. That's the only one they had left with a view of the pool."

"Nice!"

Lynn handed him the keycard as she replied, "Figured you would appreciate that. Where's Grace?"

Mikey pointed a thumb back over his shoulder. "Looking for a vending machine to punch."

Lynn nodded and then handed me my key card as she said, "That's my cue. Gentlemen, as always…"

"Thank you," I said and gave Lynn a quick parting nod, hoping she would see the sincere gratitude on my face. Whether she knew it or not, our little chat had gone a long way toward making me feel better about my current standing within the group.

Mikey and I retreated to our respective rooms to freshen up and stretch our legs, agreeing to meet at his room in an hour so we could go over the plan for tomorrow. I arrived to find Lynn and Grace already seated at a small round table by the window that was identical to the one in my room (just in case you don't know how motels work.)

Lynn smiled and gave me a little wave as I entered. Grace's right hand was clenched into a fist and she was using her left hand to hold an ice pack on it.

She briefly raised the bag so I could see her swollen knuckles as she said, "I'd wave too but I'm currently incapable."

"Wow, so Mikey wasn't joking when he said you were looking for a vending machine to punch."

"Only the ones with tempered glass fronts. Hurts like a bitch afterward but it feels so satisfying to hit them because it's glass that DOESN'T shatter, if that makes sense."

I let her words sink in and replied, "To be honest, it's actually kind of hot."

Grace did something then that I had yet to see her do; she smiled. "And if you weren't a weird scrawny man-child, that might be flattering."

Lynn shrugged at her and said, "Not bad up until then."

"I know. I'm sorry. I felt like my brain was going to induce an aneurysm if I didn't say it."

I gently clapped my hands together to get their attention (a trick I learned at magic camp, ladies) and said, "Not that this isn't a lot of fun but, uh…where the fuck is Mikey?"

As if on cue (and this time it really did happen), Mikey entered and turned to Grace as he said, "Five grand."

Grace smiled at Mikey as she gestured at me and replied, "You'll be happy to hear that you're interrupting forty-five solid seconds of polite small talk between me and…Champ over here."

I turned to Mikey and, in the most sincere tone I could muster, I said, "It WAS genuinely pleasant. I'd recommend her to all my friends."

Lynn let out a reflexive chuckle and immediately covered her mouth, looking embarrassed as Grace glared at her. Mikey was having none of our bullshit. His gaze stayed fixed on Grace as he said, "You hear me? Five grand."

Grace scoffed. "For a vending machine with a warped front? You got taken for a ride, homie."

"It's so he wouldn't call the cops, HOMIE!"

Lynn interrupted him to say, "Mikey…"

Mikey turned and abruptly smiled at Lynn and me as he said, "Sorry. Not the time. Do you have that map?"

I helped Lynn unroll the detailed map of Clear Lake she liberated from their town hall. Once we had it out on the table, Lynn quickly scanned the map and located the spot where they'd seen the old woman going into a dilapidated house earlier that day.

Mikey asked, "Was there anything strange about her? Her height or maybe an obvious deformity?"

Grace, who had seen her first, shrugged and said, "I mean, she looked like a freakin' hobo. She's obviously been squatting in that house."

Lynn added, "And that house is only accessible from a dirt bypass road leading to the quarry on the West end of the lake. Calling it out of the way would be an understatement."

I decided to chime in. "You're saying that maybe the thing that killed everybody…or took them away or whatever…it was something consciously going from house to house collecting people and simply didn't know she was there?"

Lynn nodded and said, "I mean, look. It's not even on the map so the place has obviously been condemned for a while. Plus, the tree tops would cover it if you were scanning the town from an aerial view. It's the perfect blind spot."

Mikey gently clapped his hands together (he must've gone to that same camp, gentlemen) and we all turned to look at him.

"Okay, so…Joel and I will approach at about nine tomorrow morning. We'll have to dial it in with the walkies to figure out their range but I'd like you two stationed about here…" He pointed at a spot on the far end of the other side of the map and continued, "Just outside of town."

"Bullshit," Grace said as soon as he spoke the words.

"I know that might appear overly cautious given Clear Lake's seemingly vacant status but let me remind you that we still have no idea what the fuck we're actually dealing with here. I want our bases covered. Worst case scenario, would YOU wanna saddle Lynn with Joel?"

Lynn opened her mouth as if to say something but then she decided against it and just shrugged. Grace let out a defeated sigh. "I guess not."

I turned to Mikey and said, "You realize I'm right here."

"What do you want me to say? You've had zero field experience. Which is why we're fixing that, first thing tomorrow morning."

We wrapped things up shortly after that and I must've been beat because I fell asleep pretty much as soon as I got back to my room, at which point I had one of the most terrifying nightmares I have ever experienced and if I'm the one saying that, then you KNOW it had to be bad.

4

In the dream, I understood who I was almost immediately: Jeb Casteel. A young boy terrified of his father, and rightly so. The man was a monster. Almost every night, he would stumble in, reeking of rotgut whiskey and looking to relieve the residual stress of his day by mercilessly beating Jeb. And sometimes worse. Especially after his mom passed away.

They said it was a suicide but Jeb knew better. That particular afternoon had been the final straw, though. I wasn't quite sure why exactly. All I knew was that I...Jeb...who the fuck ever couldn't take it any longer and we decided to run away, once and for all.

Jeb had no real family to speak of other than his father and nobody he could even really call a friend. At school, the gossip surrounding his father's drinking and his mother's death had made him a bit of a pariah. But what Jeb did have was one bitchin' hideout.

It was located near the south end of the lake, which was about a quarter of a mile from Jeb's backyard. The "hideout" was a repurposed drainage ditch; basically a four foot wide by eight foot deep cement-lined hole in the ground. The drainage ditches had been a holdover from back before the nearby processing facility started using the lake as a source of irrigation and its average water level had been a lot higher.

These days (the late '80s from what I could tell), the only water these ditches would be collecting was from the rain. But not Jeb's hideout; that place was bone dry. About a year ago, when he initially had the idea to convert one of them into a comfortable place to hide from his father, Jeb covered one of the ditches with a piece of plywood he had salvaged from a pile of abandoned scrap located in the woods nearby.

He picked the one with the lowest level of residual rainwater at the bottom; maybe about an inch or so. Once that had drained out through a hole in the center of the ditch's floor, Jeb used a second smaller piece of plywood to cover the bottom. The opening in the center wasn't huge but it WAS just big enough for Jeb to fit down if he jumped in longways maybe.

Still, there was really no reason to leave a hazard like that exposed if he didn't need to. Plus, the plywood beat sitting on dirty cement. The drainage ditch actually narrowed off to about three and a half feet as it neared the bottom because these things were designed to work like giant funnels. You could think of the smaller hole at the bottom as the funnel's spout. Only the hole went way deeper than it seemed was necessary.

Jeb didn't really know anything about industrial engineering, but when he was bored, he would often lift up the plywood floor and shine his flashlight down into the opening, which appeared to go on forever. This seemingly bottomless pit was the source of several of Jeb's own nightmares. Though that evening, Jeb approached his hideout to discover that a few bad dreams were currently the least of his problems.

Someone had ransacked his hideout in the two days since Jeb was there last. Whoever it had been, they cleaned him out. The crate of comic books and gaming magazines he'd stashed down there were missing, along with his manually rechargeable electric lantern/radio and even the pieces of plywood Jeb had been using as a ceiling and floor.

Though he had been coming to this exact spot almost every day for the past year and Jeb could even see the square outline of the plywood imprinted in the dirt at the bottom, he still checked just to make sure he hadn't simply approached the wrong ditch on accident. Unfortunately, that wasn't the case.

Jeb was pretty bummed about getting robbed, but it wasn't enough to outweigh the relief he felt when thinking about how he would never have to see his father again. Jeb stood at the mouth of the exposed ditch and stared down at the hollow remains of his hideout as he reminded himself that as of today, he was officially done living in fear.

He carefully mounted the first set of iron ladder rungs jutting from the inside wall and started down into the deep cement ditch, which seemed even deeper now that it was empty again. Jeb told himself he barely noticed that part as he lay down on the dirty cement floor and curled himself into a fetal position.

Jeb made a mental note to remember that he was lying only a few inches from the now-exposed spout hole and then, for some reason that he wasn't entirely sure of, Jeb began to cry...

He awoke from a dreamless sleep a few hours later to find himself suffering from a disorienting lack of vision. Jeb had never been at the ditch this late or at all without his lantern and he'd never experienced true, absolute darkness before that night. This would be an unnerving situation for most adults and, according to my sources, apparently kids are not huge fans of the dark either.

Naturally, Jeb panicked. He stood and started forward in an effort to somehow orient himself and it wasn't until he felt the world open up beneath his feet that Jeb finally remembered exactly where he had fallen asleep, but more importantly what he had fallen asleep next to.

By then, though, the opening in the center of the floor had already swallowed him whole. At least, it FELT like being swallowed. He had dropped down into the narrow space so perfectly...both legs at once and with his arms down... that it definitely didn't feel like an accident.

Much like the ditch above it, the spout also got narrower the deeper it went and Jeb didn't have to fall very far before he got stuck, arms pinned to his sides by the cramped space and about an inch of room between his nose and the slimy inside wall of the spout. Jeb spent what felt like an eternity wiggling there in the absolute darkness, straining every muscle he had to try and free himself, but it was hopeless.

Down there, hours felt like days and it seemed like a week before the sun finally rose. After it did, Jeb spent most of that first day listening intently and screaming for help whenever he heard the faintest sound or even imagined he had heard one, and sometimes even though he was sure he hadn't. When the sun eventually began to set once more, Jeb was far too dehydrated to cry, despite how much he wanted too.

That second night felt a lot longer than the first, and not just because he had to spend all of it down there this time or because of how thirsty or hungry he was. All of that was pretty shitty but the most unnerving aspect by far was the sounds Jeb kept hearing beneath him. At first, it was just scraping, like something was clawing its way up through the pipe to come get him.

But as the night wore on, Jeb started to hear what sounded like a voice speaking from the endless darkness below his dangling legs. *He couldn't quite decipher the words but whatever they were saying, it sounded like a question.*

Day two actually felt even longer than night two. Sure, the scary sounds and voices stopped as soon as dawn broke but that was hardly Jeb's biggest problem by then. He could see storm clouds forming through the ditch's exposed opening. And they KEPT forming until that afternoon when it was pretty much the only thing he could see.

The faint bit of sunlight that had managed to filter in through the clouds up to that point was now quickly fading and what little remained seemed incapable of penetrating the ditch above Jeb. He felt encapsulated by the surrounding darkness once more and it wasn't long before the voice below started up again. Only Jeb was able to hear it a lot more clearly now than the previous night. Maybe because this time, it was saying his name…

"Jeb? Juh-EB? Hey, Jeb! I'm talkin' to you here!"

"Nuh-uh! You're just a voice in my head!"

The voice began to cackle and it said, "Wouldn't that be nice!"

The inhuman laughter beneath him was enough to make Jeb literally tremble in fear but he was determined not to let it show in his own voice as he screamed back, "Yes, you are! You're a fig-mint of my 'magniation!"

Rain suddenly began to pour down on him and with Jeb's own body clogging the spout, the water draining in from the ditch above was soon up to his chin. Then it was covering his mouth. Then his nose.

When Jeb was moments from drowning, a small crevice opened in front of him. The water quickly drained away through this narrow opening, leaving a drenched Jeb to dangle there, gasping for air. The voice below him cackled once more.

"Could a figment of your imagination do THAT?"

Jeb didn't want to answer the question, so instead he asked, "Why are you doing this to me?"

"What, saving you from drowning? There's a lot more rain where that came from and you have about, oh, thirty seconds before it starts up again. But if you want me to seal the drain, I can..."

The crevice began to close and Jeb's already pounding heart was sent into overdrive by the thought of drowning again as his body began to reflexively struggle against the narrow confines holding him in place.

"No! PLEASE!" Jeb's mind raced with a thousand horrible questions. Though at that moment, there was only one that he could properly convey with words...

"Who are you?"

"That should be obvious," *the voice replied, followed by yet another evil laugh. The crevice in front of Jeb began to widen until he could see into it and he realized the opening was emitting a faint red light, almost pink. Squinting into the light, Jeb could just barely make out the shape of something...*

Something that made me, the adult male named Joel, wake up screaming like I was trying to do my best Janet Leigh impression.

Holy titty-fucking shit, WHAT WAS THAT?!

I've had a problem with chronic nightmares for most of my life, but this was something altogether new. I checked the clock on my phone and saw that I had been asleep a little more than three hours, during which time I had a dream that felt like it lasted the better part of three days. I was drenched in sweat and every muscle in my body ached. I felt utterly drained but there was no way I was going back to sleep that night.

I busted out the old laptop and started transferring that day's files from my voice recorder. I spotted the *Helpless Herman* launcher on my desktop and everything suddenly clicked as if some subconscious part of my brain had just gone. *Duh, dumbass...*

5

I told Mikey about my dream on our drive into Clear Lake that next morning and then proceeded to explain my theory of what Humbug Hill had to do with any of this and where it might be located. He listened to the dream part with an uncomfortable expression on his face and when I was just about finished detailing my theory, I concluded with…

"Basically, Jeb has returned after spending the past thirty years trapped under Clear Lake and now he's making the townspeople play a real-life version of *Helpless Herman*."

"Because that's what the Devil made him do," Mikey replied, still sounding a bit unsure.

"Exactly."

"So, the transient is a decoy and the house…"

"Is a trap, yes."

Mikey thought this over for a moment and shrugged. "Then fuck it. Let's go get trapped."

Lynn and Grace followed us to just outside of town, where both cars pulled over so we could all double check to make sure our walkies were working and on the right channel. Mikey quickly went over the bullet points of the plan one last time:

He and I were going to radio them when we were approaching the house and then if neither of us radioed back in fifteen minutes, that was their green light to go ahead with plan B, which was "save our asses and then probably a lot of running."

Mikey had advised against telling Lynn and Grace about our updated plan of approach.

He convinced me it would be a moot point and would only serve to put them on edge, "which is not where we want our back-up if we hope to maintain a consistent cover."

After making sure that everything was in order, we switched cars with them because Mikey claimed that the rental would be "more subtle" than the Porsche, which might've been okay if he hadn't also said I would be the one driving into town the previous night.

I studied that map pretty thoroughly beforehand and using the rental car's GPS, I was able to get us to the bypass road in no time. Of course, the complete lack of traffic helped. Mikey spotted the house through the trees and I slowed so I could make the turn onto the path leading to it. As per Mikey's plan, I pulled up to the front of the house and parked.

Mikey casually exited the car before retrieving a briefcase and a white Panama hat from the back seat. After radioing in that we were preparing to enter, I exited the car as well and I must've given Mikey a look as I saw him put on that hat, because he then gestured to it and said, "The point is that it's naturally disarming."

"Can't argue with you there. I see that guy coming, I'm not thinking 'this dude goes hard' so much as 'where does his improv comedy troupe meet when his mom is using the basement to host Bridge games?'"

Mikey snapped and pointed at me as he replied, "Exactly."

He and I started toward the house and as we reached the front door, Mikey gave it a rhythmic knock that somehow made him look even more hokey. After a minute or so without any sign of a response from inside, Mikey knocked more forcefully and we heard a raspy female voice shout...

"I am coming! Calm the fuck down!" The door suddenly swung open to reveal a squat toothless woman with stringy hair who said, "Is this what I think it is?"

Mikey nodded at her and replied, "Good morning, ma'am. Are you familiar with the teachings of Jesus Christ?"

I held up a Bible and added, "Good book? Try GREAT book."

The woman gave us a confused scowl and said, "I don't get it. I thought you were here to ask about him. He told me you would come when it was already too late for the others but that you would want to know about him anyway."

Mikey and I exchanged a surprised look and then finally I asked, "Are you...talking about Jeb Casteel?"

The woman's frustrated expression became one of delighted surprise. She held her hand in the universal signal for "stop in the name of love" and said, "Is THAT who Mr. Twisted is? It makes so much sense now!"

Mikey furrowed his brow at her. "Who is Mr. Twisted?"

"Would you like some coffee? I'll tell you. He said it's okay. It's why he spared me. He said, 'They will want to know what happened here, even if they couldn't possibly understand it.' It's just a long story."

Mikey and I exchanged another look and he shrugged. We followed the woman inside and through a dark foyer before finally emerging into a sunlit living room. The woman was definitely squatting. Her "kitchen" was a fold-out table next to an unrolled sleeping bag and was comprised of:

One crock pot, a plastic jug of water, and a hot plate with

an old-timey coffee brewer on it that looked like one tea kettle welded atop another.

Though the coffee that came out of those things was usually pretty decent and she even had sugar, so I couldn't complain. I thanked the woman when she handed me the steaming metal camping mug, but then Mikey signaled not to drink it as she turned to approach the empty fold-out chair across from us.

Just as she was about to sit, the woman spotted something and said, "Oh, here you go. A visual aid…"

The woman retrieved what turned out to be a PTA pamphlet from the cluttered floor and carried it back over to Mikey, who then showed it to me. The words "**BEWARE OF MR. TWISTED**" were printed on its cover, above what was labeled as an eyewitness sketch of a man with a contorted shape and scarred features.

The woman took her seat and cleared her throat as she began, "It started with just a handful of children who reported waking up to see him watching through the window of their bedroom one night. It was the third or fourth one who coined the name Mr. Twisted but they all had more-or-less the same description of him. These kids were in different grades and most of them had never even met each other. Things started to get really bad after that. More and more children were reporting sightings and then one night, he started taking people away."

The woman raised her own mug to her lips and I saw her hand tremble as she took a sip. She continued, "He spared me and I thought it was just because he wanted someone to be here to tell you what happened when you came looking for them. But now I know it's because I went to school with Jeb Casteel and I was always nice to him. I was pretty much the only one who was. Holy shit…I'm glad I did that."

Mikey asked, "What did he do with everybody else?"

The woman held up a finger. "Wait, I know the answer to this one. I'm supposed to say 'He'll show you.'"

As the woman said this, she pointed at the darkened foyer we had just entered through. There, standing hunched in the doorway, was what had become of Jeb Casteel: Mr. Twisted, in the disjointed flesh.

Mikey placed his briefcase on the floor and popped the latches open as Mr. Twisted began to lurch toward us at what was an alarmingly fast speed. The case dropped open to reveal Pasadena Guy's crystals fixed to the inside. Mikey quickly slid the "on switch" crystal into its slot at the top and then kicked the briefcase toward the nightmarish figure currently hurling itself at us.

Mr. Twisted suddenly shot up to the ceiling with a loud THWACK. He glared down at us and, realizing that he was pinned there, began to snarl.

I said, "Okay, we got him up there. Now what?"

"The first step is always identifying your target. We need to figure out what he is exactly," Mikey replied as he reached a hand around to the back of his waistband. "Abomination, demonic possession, or other."

"Do you have like a P.K.E. Meter for that or something?"

"Or something," Mikey said as he pulled out a large-caliber revolver and then fired two rounds into the gut of Mr. Twisted. The bullets tore easily through his rotted clothing and sickly gray flesh, briefly revealing entrails that seemed to be smeared with black ink. A moment later, those same bullet wounds began to heal before our eyes.

"Shit," Mikey said. "Demonically possessed abomination…that's the one I DIDN'T want it to be."

"So what do we do?"

Mikey scoffed and said, "You seen *Dark Knight*?"

6

Cut to me, Mikey, and the transient woman standing outside of the dilapidated house and watching as a fiery trail of gasoline ignited the front porch, engulfing the ancient wood almost immediately.

The woman turned to look at Mikey and then me as she said, "Thanks for not, like, burning me alive, too, even though I set you guys up and everything."

Mikey let out a somber chuckle and replied, "That's not really our style...besides, it's not like you had much of a choice."

I assumed the fire had reached the ceiling of the den by that point because we could hear Mr. Twisted cry out in what was surely an inhuman amount of pain.

I turned to the woman and said, "That reminds me. I have a few more questions about Jeb I was hoping you could answer. Was this the house he was living in when he disappeared?"

She nodded. "Yeah. His dad moved them here after his mom killed herself."

Mikey pointed at me and said, "THAT'S why it didn't match the address in the school records."

"And one more, the hideout he had by the lake...did he ever tell you what his name for it was?"

"Yeah," She said, as if recalling a very old memory for the first time in a long while. "He let me play that game he'd made during typing class. It was called the same thing...Something Hill."

Mikey retrieved the walkie from the car and let our back-up know we were okay as I began to lead us through the woods dividing the lake from the house. We had to make our way towards Clear Lake's titular attraction on foot, which is one of the aspects that made "Humbug Hill" such a perfect hideout.

We reached the lake after about fifteen minutes of hiking and I was planning on using my dream as a guide to try and locate Jeb's drainage ditch, but Mikey quickly shot out his arm to block me as I started out from the treeline.

"Look," he said and nodded forward.

The thirty or so feet of open ground bordering the shore of the lake was littered in narrow oval-shaped holes. They appeared to encircle the entire lake.

I heard what sounded like a woman crying out from one of the nearby holes, her tone weak as she shouted, "Oh god, is someone there?!"

"Yeah," I shouted back out of pure reflex. Mikey shook his head and mouthed the words, *What are you doing?*

The woman replied, "Thank you, Jesus! Oh thank you, thank you, thank you! I'm stuck in one of these fucking holes! PLEASE help me!"

I shrugged at Mikey and he slowly shook his head as I yelled, "Maybe I should go get someone! You sound like you're too far down for me to reach!"

"NO! Please don't leave me alone out here! Something comes for us at night! Something terrible! I think I'm the only one left now! The only one who still refuses to give in but if you go..."

"I'll be back before sundown, I promise!"

The woman began to laugh and then I heard her mutter, **"Screw it…"**

A sickening sound began to emanate from several of the holes at once; it was the crack of fracturing bone combined with the wet snap of tearing flesh. I felt something squeezing my arm and looked to see Mikey pulling me back into the woods as he mouthed the word, *RUN!*

We sprinted back the way we came and it wasn't long before I could see the back of Jeb's old house still burning in the distance. As we neared the raging structure fire, Mikey raised the walkie to his mouth and said, "Lynn? Shut it down."

Lynn immediately replied, "Come back with that?"

"I said SHUT IT DOWN!"

"Copy. How long do you think you're gonna need?"

We rounded the house and Mikey threw up his arms in frustration as he saw the sprinkling of safety glass where our car had been parked. Into the radio, he said, "Considering that hobo bitch jacked our car, a little longer than expected."

From the forest behind us, a chorus of steadily approaching rustling sounds began to emanate and I glanced back to see that there were now several dozen twisted silhouettes chasing us.

"Mikey, we gotta move," I said and pointed to the left. "The actual town is back that way…"

Mikey lifted the walkie and yelled, "Meet us where Main Street meets the woods in ten!"

We darted into the treeline to our left and soon the forest appeared to be vibrating behind us; an optical illusion created by the thousands of mangled figures currently pursuing

Mikey and me. We guided ourselves through a sliding run as the terrain suddenly sloped downhill before spitting us out into a sun-drenched clearing.

The momentum from our downhill slide propelled us across the clearing and into another dense patch of trees. I glanced behind us as we started back into the woods and immediately wished that I hadn't. A giant swarm of Mr. Twisteds was snaking across the sunlit clearing, writhing and shoving against one another as each fought for the space to continue crawling forward.

These abominations were more recent; their transformation had been several decades shorter and their wounds were fresher, which made the sight of them all the more disturbing. The worst part was that these fuckers seemed to be inhumanly fast and it wasn't long before I didn't have to keep glancing over my shoulder to chart their progress because I could HEAR them clawing their way through the woods directly behind us.

"I see buildings," Mikey shouted as he pointed forward but before I could even look, my attention was diverted by the sound of a descending military drone. It was gliding directly over us now, just above the tree line. Mikey checked his watch. "They're early."

That's what "shut it down" had been code for: lock on our coordinates via the GPS in Mikey's smartphone and relay those coordinates to Mikey's government contacts, who were currently standing by to call in a drone strike if need be. And "shut it down" meant that was the case.

They were supposed to wait until we were clear of the target before the drone started firebombing, but that didn't appear to be a luxury we could afford at the moment and the drone pilot must have been able to tell because he decided not to wait.

There was a flash of hot yellow light from behind us and then the world was all fire and horrific screams muffled by the heavy thud of falling trees. I have no idea how we cleared those woods alive other than to assume that the drone's remote pilot must have been one damn good shot.

When we returned to the motel, Mikey pulled me aside to say that I had done a good job for my first day out in the field and that he was proud of me. I had to control my smile so that it didn't turn into a full-on grin. The fact that my ears were still ringing and all I could smell was burning hair didn't seem to matter so much after that.

We had a "quick group rap-sesh" outside Mikey's door and then the four of us adjourned to our respective rooms to pass out, or so I thought...

7

It was just shy of midnight when I suddenly awoke to a loud knock on the door of my motel room. I groaned and finished pulling my pants on as I started over to the door. "Who is it?"

A female voice filtered in through the door with an annoyed tone to it that I immediately recognized as she said, "There's this thing called a peephole. You should try it out. All the cool kids are using 'em."

"Yeah, because that was a lot easier than just saying 'Grace,'" I replied as I pulled the door open to find her standing there, holding two large to-go cups of coffee. Grace handed me one of the coffees and nodded back toward the parking lot.

"I didn't know if you liked any of that pussy shit but there's cream and sugar in the car, just in case."

"Thanks?" I said as I accepted the cup and took a sip. I then promptly turned my head and spit it back out.

Grace nodded at me and said, "Smooth."

"You failed to mention that it was spiked with whiskey."

Grace squinted at me. "It's coffee at night. I thought that was to be assumed."

"Right, of course. Because I'm the weird one here. Who raised you, Ron Swanson?"

As I spoke the words, I recalled Lynn's comment about daddy issues and immediately regretted opening my big fat stupid mouth. There was a moment where it seemed like it could've gone either way as Grace studied my expression. Finally, she shrugged and said, "Honestly? Kind of, yeah."

I nodded at her. "I'm glad you finally got one of my references. I was genuinely starting to worry that you were an alien wearing a very convincing skinsuit."

"Just because I don't acknowledge them, doesn't mean I don't get them. By the way…" Grace pointed at me and said, "*Species*."

"Correct," I replied, genuinely impressed.

"I mean, I DO work for a guy whose legal name is a *Goonies* reference."

"Good point. So…what is THIS all about," I asked, gesturing at the coffee in my hand.

"I need you to come help me stake out Mikey's room in case I nod off."

"Uh-huh. And WHY are we staking out Mikey's room?"

"Because, Mauricio just called to tell me that he's been sending weird texts all night. He's worried Mikey is going to do something stupid and asked could we please keep an eye on him if he goes anywhere. I have a feeling Mikey had us stay here an extra night for a reason."

I followed Grace to the new rental car which showed up earlier that evening to replace the one that the homeless woman stole. Grace had parked it at the far end of the lot with the nose of the car facing out so that we had a perfect line of sight of Mikey's room. It was only a few minutes later that he exited and started toward his Porsche.

Grace kept the headlights off as we followed Mikey's car out of the parking lot and didn't turn them on until we were approaching the interstate. We drove South for about twenty minutes and then took an exit that had us going west for another thirty. Finally, Mikey took an exit labeled "Dew Well" and we followed after him at a safe distance.

Mikey led us into a residential part of town, where he eventually parked in front of a dark dilapidated house that didn't look all that different from Jeb Casteel's former home. Grace and I watched as Mikey then headed inside the house without hesitation.

Grace pulled a handgun from her purse and pulled back the slide to chamber a round as she said, "I guess we're going in."

"Does EVERYONE have a gun but me?"

Grace dug around inside her purse and retrieved a bottle of pepper spray. "You want this?"

I rolled my eyes and begrudgingly took the pepper spray. Then, for the second time in twenty-four hours, I started inside a spooky dilapidated house for reasons that I wasn't entirely sure of. Though, the fact that this time was at night made the experience even more unsettling.

Grace slowly pushed open the ajar front door, careful not to let its ancient hinges creak too loud as it swung inward. The sound of footsteps emanated down from upstairs, prompting Grace and I to start up the dusty steps to our left.

As we reached the second-floor landing, I glanced into the room across the hall and spotted Mikey standing motionless in a corner, his back to us and partially illuminated by the moonlight seeping in through the deteriorated ceiling above. I was having a flashback to the final scene of *The Blair Witch Project* but then Mikey let out a loud groan as he started to urinate.

Most of the remaining tension I was feeling quickly deflated as Mikey sighed and said, "You two might as well come in."

Grace and I looked at each other and then we started inside the remains of what appeared to be a child's bedroom. The walls in here were scorched as if the room had survived a fire. A clearly wasted Mikey zipped up his fly as he turned to then offer us the lit joint that had been dangling from his mouth.

Grace shook her head and I replied, "Well, I don't wanna be rude.`"

I took a hit from the joint and handed it back to Mikey as he slowly approached a broken window overlooking the backyard. He just stood there for a moment, silently staring down in to the overgrown grass below, and then finally Mikey said…

"The Ellis family used to run this town. Pretty much anyone who made a decent living was employed by them. Their patriarch, a bigoted old codger named Walton, had made a fortune mass-producing cheap but elegant looking furniture and when Walton died, his even more pigheaded son George took over and managed to expand the business nationwide. George had two sons. And while Georgie Jr. turned out to be a douche bag just like his old man the younger one, Sam, had been my first love."

Mikey briefly looked back to give us a sad smile and I saw that his eyes were already welling with tears as he continued his story…

8

Mikey had always known he was different, but it wasn't until he met Sam that he actually knew HOW. It was Sam who had first dubbed him Dead Things Mikey. Seeing *Goonies* in theaters when they were like fourteen had basically been their first date...the first time they kissed.

Of course, being two young boys who grew up in the South, they knew what would happen if anyone saw them. But movie theaters were a pretty safe place to make out. Especially since they usually bought tickets for the least popular movie playing or whatever had been out the longest. Anything that would guarantee them an empty theater.

Sam and Mikey were always very careful but their plan had a fatal flaw that they hadn't accounted for...

It was their senior year of high school when Georgie Junior's friend started working as a projectionist at that same theater. He spotted them making out during *Best of the Best* and it wasn't long before Sam's father found out.

That next morning, as Mikey was walking to school, Georgie Junior and one of his meathead buddies pulled up alongside him. Mikey was caught off guard at first but then he spotted the murderous intent in Georgie's eyes and took off running back to his house.

Unfortunately, Mikey's father was a lot like Jeb's had been. His sister used to swear that before their mom died, he was different. There had been some good still left in him. The fact that he worked as a floor manager for Ellis Furniture hadn't helped matters.

Mikey made it back home with Junior and his buddy still hot on his trail and there was his father, sitting in that ugly faux leather recliner he loved so much with the phone to his ear and he had this look on his face…the look of utter disappointment. Georgie Junior came barging in behind Mikey and he begged his dad to help.

That's when his father grabbed Mikey by the arm and shoved him towards the older boys and said, "Get this faggot out of my house."

Mikey said every prayer he knew while he was lying there, tied up in that flatbed with a burlap sack over his head. And considering what happened next, he just might've been listening…

When Mikey arrived at the Ellis family estate, he could hear Sam screaming and even years later, he couldn't really tell me what happened next. All Mikey remembered was them pulling that sack off of his head and him hearing Sam's screams and then suddenly it was Georgie Junior who was screaming.

The tip of his nose was missing and blood was spraying from his face and that's when Mikey realized what he was clutching between his teeth. Junior's goon took off running when he saw what Mikey had done and he proceeded to beat young Georgie to death with his bound fists.

When he was done, Mikey followed Sam's screaming to a field behind the house. He spotted a massive bonfire set up near a big oak tree and there was Sam, hanging from that tree. He was beaten half to death himself and both of his eyes were nearly swollen shut but somehow he saw Mikey approaching and even managed to smile.

The big fucker standing beneath Sam yanked on the rope feeding to the noose around his neck, snapping it like a twig and killing him right there while Mikey was sprinting toward him. It made the most awful sound and yet Sam died with a grin on his face.

Mikey rushed the man holding the rope and shoved him headlong into the bonfire. Once the poor bastard managed to pull himself out, he took off screaming with his clothes engulfed in flames. Mikey was crouched down beside Sam's limp body, trying to get him to open his eyes, to say something...

When he was tackled from behind by Georgie Senior. The old man had apparently found what remained of his eldest son out front because he started choking Mikey and screaming, "What did you do to Georgie?!"

His knees were on Mikey's shoulders, pinning him down. His vision started to go and soon after, Mikey saw himself lifting up out of his body. And that's when he spotted it...the demon standing over Georgie Senior, stroking its massive thorny erection.

At the time, Mikey didn't know anything about corporeal versus discorporeal or that when a human soul first leaves its host body, it is in a transcorporeal form. All he understood in this strange new state of being was that he wanted revenge for Sam and before he realized what he was doing, Mikey floated over to that demon and bit down on the head of his big red dick.

He had no way of knowing the resulting surge of energy the

demon emitted to get him to let go would also force Mikey's soul back into his body or that this same surge would transfer to Georgie Senior, exploding his heart and killing him instantly. But anyway, that's what happened...

"That was the night I learned there was more to this world than what we can see with our eyes. That there were terrifying things all around us but they were also things that one could use to their advantage IF they knew the right buttons to push."

After a final pause, Mikey turned to face us as he concluded his tale...

"Perhaps Sam was aware of the evil that had been leeching off of his family's greed and hatred for the past several generations; I'm not sure. But he certainly knew what they were capable of and had even planned for just such an outcome. Georgie Senior had a personal net worth in the hundreds of millions and Sam stood to inherit half of that fortune upon his father's death. And about six months before Sam was murdered, he had seen a lawyer and drafted a will that made me the primary beneficiary of Sam's estate, which essentially made his inheritance mine. That money was the reason I got to travel the world, searching for answers to all of the questions I had after that night. Sam's money allowed me to make the contacts I needed to become the Dead Things Mikey you two now know and love so much that you'll stalk him to a town in the middle of bumfuck nowhere just to hear his sob story."

Grace opened her mouth to reply but then she hesitated as if considering not to before finally asking, "Did you ever see your father again?"

Mikey smirked at her and jabbed a thumb back over his shoulder as he said, "Who do you think I was peeing on?"

We heard a rustling in the far corner of the room and then a weathered voice shouted, "What smells like fresh piss?!"

Mikey turned to face the corner and shouted back, "That'd be you, you dirty fucking hobo!"

An old man with a beard and long stringy hair leaned out from the darkness and said, "Michael?"

"Hey, Dad. You hungry?"

Mikey took the three of us out to eat at a greasy roadside diner and, needless to say, it was a pretty awkward dinner until his father asked where Mikey's "little caramel man" was and we all started laughing. Mikey and his dad had an interesting dynamic, to say the least, and listening to their back-and-forth had been downright adorable.

Grace unconsciously placed her hand on mine as we were laughing at yet another one of Mikey's dad's quaintly insensitive comments. Quickly realizing what she had just done, Grace retracted her hand. She looked at me and something seemed to dawn on her then.

Grace turned to Mikey and said, "You told Mauricio to call me, didn't you?"

With a guilty smile, Mikey looked at Grace and replied, "Maybe…"

Grace scoffed as she slowly shook her head. "How did you know I'd bring Joel?"

Mikey shrugged. "Lucky guess…plus, I told Lynn to turn off her cell and Mauricio to subtly suggest that you take a partner on your stake-out."

Grace emitted a frustrated groan as she turned to me and

said, "We work for a conniving motherfucker. I hope you know that."

I was well aware.

Part 3

CASE FILE #2: "Why Dead Things Mikey Always Gets Paid Upfront"

1

Scuddy Ratner was the kind of guy who could make you believe in magic. I, for one, was fairly certain he was the result of some *Weird Science*-style dimensional rift which had inadvertently given flesh to the villain from an overly zealous feminist comic strip because people like Scuddy didn't actually exist in the real world, right?

I mean, what grown man comes to the door wearing nothing but an open silk bathrobe and boxers when HE was the one who invited you over? It had to be an act because if that was appropriate wear for company, what was the dress code at *Casa de Ratner* when Scuddy was home alone, nipple clamps and a cocktail umbrella up his urethra?

And what a home it was, too: a large stucco McMansion that just screamed new money. Though, according to Scuddy, that wasn't entirely true. Apparently, his family had been loaded and he'd used his sizable trust fund as the startup capital for what eventually became a lucrative online porn empire. Scuddy was just tacky.

He had designed the whole place himself, floor-to-ceiling. The ultimate bachelor pad for the self-proclaimed "ultimate bachelor…like Clooney before he pussied out."

Scuddy was also in the habit of dating women more than half his age. Shocker, I know. They were mostly girls "in the biz" as he would put it with a lecherous grin that looked alarmingly comfortable on his pudgy, cherub-like face. The morning in question had begun very much like any other...

Scuddy awoke to find himself staring at a pair of spray-tanned breasts so blatantly fake that they seemed to defy all laws of god and man. Eventually, he glanced up at the face of the girl sleeping in his bed. Not bad. A little stupid looking but that was how Scuddy liked 'em.

From the right angle, though, this one was actually rather pretty, despite the smear of dried blood beneath her nose which perplexed Scuddy. He didn't remember her getting mouthy the previous night. Probably from all the coke then. It had been some pretty good shit.

He slowly sat up and climbed out from under the covers, moving carefully so as not to wake Miss Bloodynose Orangetits. Scuddy stood and preemptively shielded his eyes with his hand as he pulled open the long row of blinds covering the sliding glass door beside his bed, revealing a sunlit expanse of backyard complete with a large pool and adjacent hot tub.

With his eyes still covered, Scuddy started outside and trudged across the small balcony that anchored a set of narrow wooden stairs to the side of his house. As per Scuddy's morning ritual, he then lowered his boxers and began to urinate off the side of the balcony.

The stream arched to hit its usual patch of rancid dead grass that had begun to form in the yard below. Scuddy noted that the patch was getting pretty big as he shook the last drops of urine loose and shrugged. What could he do?

The master bath was all the way on the other side of his bedroom, which was already big enough that he risked getting winded just crossing it. Scuddy wasn't about to make that hike every morning just to drain the main vein. He had briefly considered moving his bed but didn't feel like dealing with the hassle of having to mount another mirror on the ceiling.

As Scuddy bent to pull up his boxers, he heard a noise overhead that made him picture a flying sewing machine. He glanced up to see a delivery drone slowly descending on his house. It was a model similar to the type Amazon used but Scuddy immediately recognized the logo on its side as a drone from his own fleet.

One of Scuddy's more profitable side ventures had been a discreet sex toy delivery service called "Tilde." His business manager, Ross, had actually given it the name. Scuddy wanted to call the business "Jack of None" because he was…

"Pretty much the king of everything and plus our clients are folks sick of jackin' their stuff the old fashioned way, so it works on two levels."

Ross took a moment to think and then he said, "Remember, the key to this one is that it's a DISCREET delivery service. That's a pretty brazen name."

"Then what about no name at all? We could pull a Prince and call it something stupid like a symbol."

"Interesting idea. What did you have in mind?"

Scuddy shrugged but then immediately snapped his fingers and grabbed Ross's open laptop, spinning it around to face his side of the desk. He began to type with a devilish smirk on his face and, after a few quick keystrokes, Scuddy turned the laptop back to reveal an open Word doc displaying a single line of text…

B=====D~~~

"Perfect, right?"

"So perfect. And super subtle. Can I just…make one TINY revision?" Ross said and slid his laptop back across the desk. He held down backspace until all that remained of the symbol was one lonely squirt of jizz…

Ross let out a weary sigh and corrected Scuddy. "It's not jizz. It's a tilde."

Sure, at the time, Scuddy had been a little underwhelmed by the choice, but as it turned out, Ross actually knew his shit. He had been right about a discreet name being great for business and when it came to weird charges showing up on a credit card statement, "Tilda INC." was about as discreet as it got.

Scuddy had actually never been on the other end of the delivery process before that morning and though he was a little confused by what the drone was doing at his house, he was quite pleased with how far out he was able to spot that white squiggle on the side. The potential for brand recognition with this one was so overwhelming, Scuddy was worried he was going to "tilde" just thinking about it.

Then Scuddy finally realized what the drone was carrying and his exposed chub went from "half mast" to "shy turtle head" so quickly that, had anyone been there to witness it, they would've thought he was rehearsing the world's saddest magic trick.

But, for possibly the first time in his life, Scuddy's biggest concern wasn't the state of his erection. At that moment, he was too busy trying not to scream as he stood there with a hand over his agape mouth and his wide eyes fixed on the descending delivery drone. Situated awkwardly in the drone's claw machine-like grasp, was a woman's dismembered torso.

The drone gingerly placed its macabre cargo down on the deck beside Scuddy, who examined the nude torso with a look of confused disgust. There was a sudden sharp *whurring* sound that startled Scuddy as the drone released the torso and zipped off, ascending more than a hundred feet into the air before it eventually disappeared into an approaching storm cloud while a dumbfounded Scuddy just stood there and watched.

2

See, when this sort of thing happens to people as rich as Scuddy, they don't call the police. The line of questioning that would lead to would be stressful enough for your average Joe but for someone as wealthy as him, it could be downright catastrophic. Scuddy had known far better men who lost everything over less. Which is why when shit got real for people like him, they called guys like Dead Things Mikey.

"And what did you do with the torso itself?" Mikey was asking Scuddy as I glanced away from the oval stain on his deck and turned to give the yard behind us a cursory scan. There wasn't a fence around it but we were in Covington, where that was to be expected. "Across the lake" as us N.O. natives knew it.

The area was quite rural but a good portion of its residents were affluent types like Scuddy who conducted their weekly business in the city and then commuted all the way across Lake Pontchartrain just so they wouldn't have to live there as well. Of course, we're talking about the kind of people who could afford to commute via helicopter.

If you happened to be a broke chump like the other 99% of us, your only option was to take the Huey P. Long Bridge both ways and no, I'm not trying to make you my patsy in a crank call. Someone actually named their child "Huey P. Long" and then somebody else named a bridge after him.

"I got the torso in a cold storage freezer in my shed with the rest of the pieces."

Mikey opened his mouth to respond but then he paused, looking as if he were trying to fully process this new bit of information without his brain hemorrhaging from the sudden influx of stupid.

Finally, Mikey replied, "There are MORE pieces?"

"Yeah. Five so far, including the torso. A thigh, an arm. The last one was just like her…"

Scuddy lowered both hands to his groin and waved them in small circles as he continued, "Crotchal region?"

I gave him a pandering nod and said, "Sure."

"I didn't actually see the drone deliver most of 'em but once after that first time, I could HEAR it. I think it knew I had my gun on me because no matter where I moved to, I couldn't get a line of sight on the fucker. That time, it brought a whole arm. Thing rolled down off the roof and landed right there."

Scuddy pointed at where I was standing on the balcony as he added, "Scared the shit out of me…"

"Do all of the pieces appear to be female?" Mikey asked but then, before Scuddy could answer, he added, "Can you bring us to that freezer?"

"Yeah, it's over at the guest house. Come see," Scuddy said as he waved for us to follow him down the balcony stairs. "And yeah, they're all girl parts."

3

Scuddy led us to the guest house located at the other end of his property, and then around back to a discreet-looking shed (which was bigger than my entire apartment, so when I say "shed," keep that in mind.)

Against the far wall of the shed sat a large industrial freezer, the kind that had a lid instead of a door and was sort of shaped like a really thick coffin. Its compressor was purring along with a loud hum that said, *I don't fuck around.*

Scuddy lifted the freezer lid to reveal the body parts he had listed earlier resting atop a space still half packed with boxes of bagel bites and gallon-sized ice cream containers. I pointed down at the food and said, "You're not going to eat any of that, right?"

Scuddy shrugged and replied, "I mean not the stuff it's touching."

Mikey flashed a look that told me he'd just about reached his daily limit of Scuddy and then he turned to smile at the man as he said, "Would you mind giving us a minute? This next part isn't pretty and we're going to need our space to get set up."

"Say no more." Scuddy gave him a dismissive wave and then gestured at an old refrigerator against the wall to our left as he said, "There's beer and soda in the fridge. Help yourself. No body parts in that one, I promise."

Scuddy winked at me when he said this and I pointed a

thumb back behind us as I responded, "So it's just the freezer then? That IS comforting. Thanks."

I thought the smile on my face said, *This is just a friendly jest.*

Based on his reaction, though, Scuddy heard my face say something more along the lines of, *When you die alone, I will mouth-fuck your corpse.*

His expression, which went from tender levity to bitter disappointment in a single moment, was enough to make me start to question my initial judgment of Scuddy as a brazen prick who didn't care what people thought of him. I was also starting to suspect he might have a touch of Asperger's.

After a tense moment of silence, Scuddy finally recovered from my perceived slight enough to nod toward his house as he said, "Well…you fellas take all the time you need. I'll be inside watching the game."

Once Scuddy had left the shed and Mikey was certain that he was out of earshot, he looked at me and erupted into laughter as I slowly shook my head.

"Come on! That was some straight-up Larry David shit."

"It's not funny. I'm pretty sure that guy's mildly autistic."

Mikey let out another chuckle as he placed a hand on my shoulder and replied, "It's sweet of you to say 'mildly'…you have that tarp and the gloves?"

I nodded and reached into my computer bag, retrieving a package containing a tightly folded plastic sheet and a box of extra-thick latex gloves.

Mikey gestured at the floor and said, "Can you lay it out for me? I'm gonna need a minute to sort through this mess."

I handed him the box of gloves and said, "Sure."

Mikey dug out a pair and tossed the box back to me. He pulled on each glove with an audible snap and then turned to approach the open freezer. Mikey glared down at its contents and slowly shook his head.

"Lonely flower…"

"What?"

Mikey had muttered the words and I wasn't quite sure I heard him correctly over the rustling of the tarp I was laying out. He reached inside and lifted the frozen torso with a faint grunt, resting it on the freezer's brim so that the back was facing toward me.

"Observe the *Cunnus Notae*…" Mikey said, pointing at the small tattoo right above where the woman's buttocks would have been. "Her tramp-stamp. They're Chinese characters. *Gudu… Hua…*"

He pointed at them again and explained, "Lonely…flower…which would actually be written as *Gūdú de huāduǒ* but you get the point."

"What does it mean?"

"Aside from a friendless species of flora? My guess is as good as yours." Mikey waved me over to the freezer and said, "You wanna give me a hand laying all this out?"

I managed to repress an initial surge of queasiness and narrowed my eyes at Mikey as I replied, "You just had to say 'hand,' didn't you?"

We set the frozen torso onto the tarp first and laid it down on its back. We then arranged the remaining pieces into what would've been their corresponding locations had they all come from the same body though from what we could tell, that didn't seem to be the case. Because what this gig really needed was to get even creepier.

When we were finally done trying to put together the world's most disturbing jigsaw puzzle, Mikey had me use my phone to snap a few pictures of the "lonely flower" tattoo. Once I had several shots I was happy with, I texted them to Grace who had spent the past day at a nearby hotel with Lynn, helping her data mine the shit out of Scuddy.

Then Mikey did something REALLY surprising…

He told me I could head back to the hotel as well and take the rest of the evening off. "Tell the girls to do the same. Order some room service. Get a movie on Pay-Per-View. Whatever you want. It's on me."

"Not to look a gift Mikey in the mouth, but are you sure?"

"Yeah, this one's looking like it's going to be pretty open and shut."

I glanced down at the tarp covered in body parts and said, "It DOES?"

"Joel…"

"Good point. I'll just take the keys to the Porsche, then."

"I ordered you an Uber while you were photographing the tattoo."

"You monster."

Mikey didn't tell me directly about what happened after I left but luckily I had been using the pen part of my pocket pen recorder to pretend like I was taking notes when we first got there because I feel like it makes me appear more useful to the client.

Anyway, my dumb ass had left the pen in Scuddy's living room when we went out onto the back deck and according to what I heard on there, shortly after I left, Mikey entered and said...

4

TIME: 7:04PM

LOCATION: Ratner Residence–Covington, LA

MIKEY:
"Shut off the TV."

[There is an audible scoff from Scuddy.]

SCUDDY:
"Excuse me?"

MIKEY:
"I told you to shut off the TV."

[A tense pause, during which the TV remains on.]

SCUDDY:
"Look, faggot…I don't care how many senators' daughters you've exorcised. You need to be careful how you talk to a man in his own home."

MIKEY:
"You need to be careful who you call faggot, you pudgy little prick. As it stands, this one has roughly four inches and fifty pounds of muscle on you and he isn't above smacking mouthy bitches who don't know when to shut their mouth and listen!"

[Another tense pause, followed by the sound of the TV turning off and Scuddy's ass resuming contact with his leather couch.]

MIKEY:

"When you do this as long as I have, there aren't very many surprises. You know how to spot most of the patterns before they've even started."

SCUDDY:

"What the fuck are you talking about?"

MIKEY:

"You don't hear that?"

[A chorus of clicking noises suddenly swells as if surrounding the room.]

SCUDDY:

"Jesus! How many are there?!"

MIKEY:

"Enough, I'm sure. It's finished toying with you by now. What you're hearing outside is called the escalation stage. Now tell me, Scuddy. What have you done?"

SCUDDY:

"What do you mean? NOTHING! I didn't do a goddamn thing! I'm paying you to help me!"

MIKEY:

"No, you're paying me for answers. I decide based on those

answers whether or not I WANT to help you. That was the deal you signed."

SCUDDY:
"Fuck you."

MIKEY:
"What did you do, Scuddy?"

SCUDDY:
"Go fuck yourself."

MIKEY:
"Have it your way. Wait out the clock. See what that gets you. In the meantime, here's an interesting factoid. You know how Catholics have a saint for everything? There are demons like that too. The Demon of Plagues, the Demon of War, the Demon of Spurned Love…"

[Mikey follows that last one with an ominous pause.]

MIKEY:
"As a for-instance, the Demon of Spurned Love? That's actually one I deal with a lot."

SCUDDY:
"What is the point of this retarded bullshit?"

MIKEY:
"The point is say you love someone, like truly love someone who actively made you believe they loved you too and that they cared for you and would protect you and then they do

something awful like have you killed and your body dissolved in lye to, say, avoid a costly divorce settlement…and you feel so utterly betrayed that you're willing to leverage your very soul for vengeance. Can you imagine that, Scuddy? Can you imagine what you would DO to someone who did that to you? The lengths you would go to in order to make them hurt as much as you? That's where the Demon of Spurned Love comes in. That one is a real doozy, too. Very creative. It reanimates the corpse of the aforementioned spurned love to take their bloody revenge by the light of the next full moon and if, for whatever reason, there isn't a corpse to reanimate then it makes one for them…"

[There is an audible crack in Scuddy's voice as he responds.]

SCUDDY:
"Out of what?"

MIKEY:
"Whatever it can find lying around, I suppose. I mean, I've seen it use all sorts of stuff. Like I said, very creative, this one. But mostly it just uses parts from other dead people."

[At this point, the doorbell begins to ring. There is a quick rustling sound from Scuddy's end of the room and Mikey's stern tone shifts suddenly, sounding almost disappointed.]

MIKEY:
"Really, Scuddy? Now, what do you think THAT is going to do for you?"

SCUDDY:

"Fuck you! You were supposed to help me! You're just fucking with me! Trying to get inside my head!"

MIKEY:
"If there's anyone fucking with you here, it's Tilde...holy shit, Scuddy! PLEASE point that somewhere else."

SCUDDY:
"What'd you say about Tilde?!"

MIKEY:
That's the demon's name...Tilde, the Lonely Flower. Usually, it will show itself somehow to the cursed beforehand. As a form of warning or maybe just validation. Scuddy, please lower that..."

5

Their voices had been steadily fading and by that point, I could no longer decipher what they were saying through the recording. Luckily, I had realized I left behind the pen-recorder when we were only about a mile away and promptly told the Uber driver we needed to turn around, because I definitely wasn't calling Mikey to ask him to grab the absurdly expensive device I'd forgotten and which he had bought me.

Eventually, I stopped ringing the doorbell and started around to the backyard to see if Mikey was still in the shed behind the guest house. I got about as far as the stilts holding up the balcony attached to Mikey's bedroom when a swarm of delivery drones suddenly exploded out from behind the guest house, halting me in my tracks.

The drones quickly dispersed and then disappeared into the night. I heard Mikey's voice and glanced up at the balcony above me where I spotted him exiting through the open sliding glass door with his hands raised.

Mikey's tone was eerily calm as he said, "I wouldn't be so willing to step outside right now if I were you, Scuddy. Not exactly the best idea, given the circumstances."

Mikey looked more annoyed than worried as Scuddy exited behind him. He was pointing a 9MM Glock at my boss and screaming, "I think it's a GREAT idea! If she's out here, then show me. Where is she, huh?"

"You don't see her?" Mikey asked, gesturing in front of them with one of his raised hands.

I saw her. A pale figure with long stringy hair was lumbering out from behind the guest house. She was the kind of pale that was usually reserved for dead people and when I say lumbering, I mean this chick had a full-on pirate limp due to the fire poker making up most of her right leg. One of her arms was twisted back in a weird position and I realized they were both lefts.

Her head was all wrong, as well. The eyes bugged out and it was far too bloated from decomposition to look right on such a slender frame. As a result, the head hung lopsided from her neck, giving the poor girl a slight hunchback. She looked like she was wearing a particularly convincing Halloween mask. But her smile…

Her smile was easily the worst part. Her teeth had been replaced with what appeared to be an assortment of tiny sharp object: nails, screws, shards of glass, the head from a scalpel…and all of it was perfectly aligned to force her mouth into this horrid grin that only got worse the longer you stared at it.

I had to take a few steps back not to block her path as the thing shambled toward me way too quickly for someone with a fire poker for a leg and then scaled up the wooden stilt I had been standing beside with a rhythmic *thud-thud-thud-THUNK* that was truly unsettling.

I followed her up with my gaze and watched as Mikey stepped aside so the mangled thing could reach over the balcony railing and grab a petrified Scuddy by his outstretched hand, the one still holding the Glock.

Scuddy squeezed the trigger and I watched a round tear clean through the back of her bloated head, but the lopsided thing just laughed. She pulled him toward her, planted a kiss on his terrified face, and then yanked Scuddy over the side of the balcony so that he landed face-down in his own festering puddle of urine.

The thing pounced down on top of him and I looked up at Mikey, pointing back toward the front of the house. "Should we…"

"This does seem like a personal matter."

"Yeah, I mean we don't know both sides. Probably better if we don't get involved."

I had waved off the Uber driver when I returned to the front of the house and greeted Mikey at the door a few moments later. As we started toward his Porsche, Mikey very casually handed me my pen recorder.

"Do try to be more careful with this."

"Sure thing, boss," I replied, taking the device and sliding it into my shirt pocket.

"You should save that file, though. Label it: Why I Always Get Paid Up Front."

Part 4

CASE FILE #3-A: "Dead Things Mikey and the Homunculus Among Us"

1

The Beverly was a sad place. You could tell that just from look-ing at it. A persistent southern Louisiana sun had faded the homely three-story building's once pink stucco exterior to a dull salmon hue which gave the hotel a look like you were viewing it through an old photograph, though that particular effect wasn't limited to just the outside.

The entire hotel had an anachronistic vibe to it. Especially the front lobby which, with its wood-paneled walls and poorly-filtered cigarette smoke, felt like a place unstuck in time. I followed Lynn across the sparsely-lit room and over to a front counter that was currently being manned by a cute girl with short blonde hair who couldn't have been older than twenty.

"Checking in?" she asked as we neared the counter, the girl keeping her big blue eyes trained on the open laptop in front of her.

Lynn replied, "No, actually we're..."

The girl abruptly cut her off as she said, "Looking for the entrance to the bar? Hallway to your left. Follow the video poker machines and you can't miss it."

She pointed toward the hallway in question, using a hand so covered in gothic looking jewelry that her arm rattled with the gesture. Lynn raised an eyebrow at the girl's accessories and said, "It is 9 AM."

I leaned between them, getting the girl's attention as I interjected, "We're here to speak with the owner, August Mayor."

"Oh shit, wait…" The girl paused the YouTube video she was watching and then leaned in close to me as she whispered, "Are you the ghost hunters?"

I glanced around, giving the empty room an exaggerated scan as I whispered back, "Not exactly."

"Hey, guys…" Mikey shouted and we turned to see him standing in the lobby's open doorway. "I found 'em."

Mikey led us back out and around to a small, unkempt courtyard hidden behind the hotel where Grace and a middle-aged man were seated on a bench opposite a short stone pedestal displaying a nine-inch angel figurine made from bundles of thin wire. Grace had already started going through the prerequisite list of questions required in this type of case which appeared to be your typical bog-standard haunting:

Guests and employees feeling uncomfortable as if they were "being watched," shadows moving in people's peripheral vision, bumps in the night…all that fun stuff.

And August, who seemed to be a nice enough fellow despite looking like he hadn't slept more than two full hours in the past two weeks, was trying his best to provide the answers. See, despite her flawless exterior, Grace wasn't exactly the best interviewer but Mikey insisted that she "hone her skills wherever possible."

"Okay, so like before your wife…SHIT." Grace retracted the smartphone she had been holding uncomfortably close to August's mouth and tapped the screen as she said, "Sorry, forgot to hit the stupid button."

August gave her a polite smile and replied, "It's quite all right."

Grace jabbed the phone back towards his face and said, "So these reports didn't start until after your wife's death?"

August nodded. "Correct."

"And the cause?"

He shrugged and replied, "I'm not sure. That's why you're here."

"No, your wife. Like how'd she die?"

"Ah…stabbed herself in the heart with a soldering iron."

"Fuck," was Grace's wide-eyed response.

As we neared the bench, I turned to Lynn and quietly muttered, "It's like watching a young Barbara Walters."

Grace reached an arm back and blindly swatted at me with impressive precision. I barely had enough time to cup my junk before she backhanded my groin like a pimp silencing the merchandise.

In that same moment, she smiled at August and replied, "I'm so sorry."

He turned to stare at the wire angel figurine in front of them and said, "Don't be. Yours was the appropriate reaction…of course, my poor, sweet Beverly hadn't been anywhere near her right mind by then. She suffered from early onset A.D."

"Oh…okay," Grace replied, though her tone was uncertain.

"Alzheimer's Disease."

"Oh!" Grace said with a knowing nod.

I'm not going to pretend like I knew what August meant either or that I didn't briefly think the man's wife had been a victim of early onset Erectile Dysfunction. But that's also probably why Mikey doesn't have me ask the questions.

"That must've been…" Grace said and then paused to reconsider her words as she slowly shook her head. "My grandfather had Alzheimer's."

"Then you have some idea of how difficult it can be."

"Oh, it was a fucking nightmare. Here was the greatest, toughest man I'd ever known reduced to this paranoid mess who would wake up at three in the morning to nail his bedroom windows shut and scream at my grandmother for being a government spy."

This made August laugh which, from the uneasy sound of it, was something he hadn't done in a long time. Grace seemed pleased by his reaction and added, "Once, he assaulted the mailman for being a communist sympathizer."

August's laughter intensified and then faded to a sigh as he said, "I apologize. It's just that…I can relate. My Beverly was an artist. Her specialty had been pieces like that one."

He gestured toward the angel figurine and for the first time, I noticed just how intricately detailed it was for something composed of what appeared to be nothing more than spools of metal wire. I could make out the features of the angel's face, her nose and her eyes, the individual rows of feathering on the wings…it seemed almost TOO detailed. I tried to calculate just how many hours it would take for a single pair of human hands to make something so intricate and just looking at the figurine started to give me an eerie feeling. I gratefully returned my attention to August as he continued his story.

"At one point, she had pieces selling for five figures. People who didn't know any better always assumed I called her a co-owner of the Beverly because she was my wife and its name-sake but the truth is she put up half the initial capital for this place. When she got sick, though, her art became her sanctuary, which would've been fine if it hadn't also become significantly more disturbing."

"How so?" Grace asked, sounding genuinely intrigued.

August let out a weary sigh and replied, "It's easier if I just show you."

2

He directed us down a narrow dirt footpath that led into the woods behind the courtyard and eventually to a beautiful two-story house hidden just a few yards past the treeline.

As the house came into view, August glanced back at us and said, "We had this built here because as much as my wife claimed she didn't want to live where she worked, she wanted our guests to know that we were always just a short walk away if they needed us."

The treetops overhead broke up the early morning sunlight into a golden patchwork of tiny malformed halos that littered the sloped roof of the house and reflected off its large bay windows as we neared, giving the place an inviting almost ethereal appearance.

"It's a beautiful home," Grace said in the awkward pause that followed as August stopped to stare at the house.

He slowly turned to look at Grace and said, "After her mind really started to go, Bev had to be confined to it for her own safety. And as shameful as this is to admit, I spent as little time here as possible after that. She had the homecare nurse to tend to her and I'd check in at least a couple times a day to see that vacant look in her eyes, the complete lack of recognition on my wife's face whenever she saw me. It broke my heart every time…I haven't been inside since her death."

That much was obvious as we got closer to the house. The front door hadn't been opened in so long that it was swollen against the jam and August had to shove himself against it before the thing finally swung inward, exposing a dimly lit foyer.

A musty smell wafted out from the house and one of the same halos of sunlight that had made the place seem so inviting from the outside shone through the open doorway to reveal that the air was thick with swirling dust.

August looked back at us, briefly scanning each of our faces, and then started inside as he said, "There was a brief period, maybe two or three months after Beverly's diagnosis, when she was still lucid enough to know what was happening to her. That time was the worst by far."

The foyer led into what I assumed was supposed to be a living room judging from the home's layout, though the complete lack of furniture and the fact that practically every corner of the space was brimming with sculptures and wire figurines made it difficult to know for sure.

"They say the final stage of grief is acceptance like it's a good thing." August scoffed and continued, "You wanna know what I think? Acceptance is overrated. Beverley told me something in her changed the day she finally accepted her fate. 'Like losing a vital part of my humanity' was how she put it. And that was when her work took a dark turn…"

We would be here all day if I attempted to accurately describe every piece in that room but if I had to sum up the collection as a whole with one unifying characteristic, it would be, "Seriously fucked up. Like, seriously."

The biggest work of the bunch encompassed the room's entire far wall. It was what pretentious art snobs like myself would classify as an "instillation."

The main focal point of the piece was a painting of a giant slug monster rearing back to reveal what I can only describe as a cavernous vulva lining its slimy underbelly. The canvas it was painted on even contained a physical slit down the center, just in case you were hoping it wasn't exactly what you thought it was. From this slit protruded a large cluster of opaque white spheres that had been suspended from the ceiling using fishing line.

I noticed several small digital projectors on a wheeled cart in the corner that were pointed at the installation and my inner A/V nerd was instantly drawn to them. I checked to make sure the projectors were hooked up and then pointed at the cart.

"You mind if I turn these on?"

August gave me a somber smile and replied, "I don't really like messing with any of this stuff. I'm not even sure those projectors still work."

"The Mac Mini they're plugged into is still running," I said, gesturing at a shelf beneath the projectors.

I could sense the hesitation in his words but the whole setup had me genuinely intrigued. Plus, this was exactly the kind of stuff we needed to be examining in detail if we planned on helping August with his present situation.

He knew it, too. I hadn't stumbled upon his dead wife's artwork by accident. The man brought us here. I could sense a similar internal monologue playing out in August's head as well and he eventually let out a weary sigh.

"Yeah, sure," August said.

He then turned to exit the room as I switched on the projectors and uncapped their lenses. I glanced back at the others and the four of us shared a moment of genuine tension in the time it took everything to warm up. Then suddenly I understood why August had left the room.

The cold lifeless faces of several dozen dead infants were now being projected onto the suspended cluster of spheres, creating what appeared to be the world's creepiest grapevine protruding from the vagina-slug painting and in that moment, all you can do is wonder, *How does someone even acquire photos of that many dead babies?*

I bent down to switch on the set of computer speakers positioned on either side of the Mini and was immediately greeted by a chorus of crying infants.

I turned to see Grace and Lynn staring awkwardly down at the floor as a wide-eyed Mikey said, "Um, Joel?"

"Yeah, that's enough of that," I responded and began to switch everything off.

When I was done, Lynn blinked a few times and then turned to Mikey as she quietly muttered, "You can see what this is, right?"

Mikey scoffed and nodded, his eyes still scanning the instillation as he said, "I can."

I glanced at Grace and she shrugged, looking just as lost as me. By this point, though, I had learned that with Mikey, it was better to simply wait for him to explain stuff when and if necessary. And the "if" was an especially vital component in that equation. Trust me.

Probably the best advice I had ever been given on the subject came from Grace:

It was about a month after I started working for Mikey. He called me at 7 AM to pick up a Duffle bag of spare clothes he had stashed at Grace's place. She was waiting outside with the bag when I pulled up and when I asked her what this was all about, Grace shrugged in much the same way as she had just now and said:

"I didn't ask. I never ask with Mikey. There are things in this world so awful that you don't know how badly you don't wanna know about them. Mikey knows about a lot of those things. If you're really smart, you won't ever ask him how."

After that, I drove to an area just outside of the city called Kenner, Louisiana and the place's glassy-eyed locals and suburban plight facade gave me the impression that I wasn't the only one who had arrived here following a set of vaguely ominous directions.

Eventually, I located the Burger King where I was supposed to park, and a few minutes later, Mikey leaned out from behind a fenced-off dumpster. He spotted my car and came sprinting over, covered in blood and completely naked save for a ratty pair of old dress shoes.

As he slid into the passenger seat, forever ruining my car's interior, Mikey pointed down at the aforementioned shoes and said, "Won these bare-knuckle boxing a homeless Mexican man. Nicest guy. Guess what his dog's name was? Mikey!"

That was the entirety of Mikey's explanation for how he had ended up this way but, taking Grace's advice to heart, I simply nodded down at my own shoes and said, "That's cool...I got these from the mall."

Back at the house behind the Beverly, Lynn pointed at Mikey and said, "Let's you and I finish questioning Mr. Mayor. Grace and Joel, will you grab the EMF detectors I set out and do a sweep of the hotel itself? They should be calibrated by now."

"Sounds like a plan," I replied. "You want me to start mounting the cameras while we're at it?"

Mikey shook his head and then nodded at the slug monster painting as he said, "Don't bother. I think we have a pretty good idea what's going on here."

3

We made our way back down the path to the hotel and retrieved the EMF detectors from the lobby where Grace and I were greeted by the same young girl from earlier, now looking nearly giddy with interest as she saw us enter.

The girl quickly rounded the counter, holding up a keycard as she said, "Mr. Mayor called and told me I was to take you guys through all of the rooms so you could scan for ghosts."

I smiled at the girl, my tone polite as I said, "I'm sorry. What's your name?"

"Carol Anne but everybody except my mom just calls me Annie." She handed me the key card and said, "That's programmed to be a skeleton key. It'll open any door in here that has a magnetic lock."

"Thanks," I replied and then held up the EMF detector. "So, Annie, what this device does is it detects fields emitted by electromagnetic objects."

"What does that mean?"

I looked at the device in my hand and said, "To be honest, Annie, I'm not entirely sure. What I do know is that even when properly calibrated, a number of very typical everyday things can set them off."

"So not just ghosts?"

Grace slowly shook her head and let out a tired sigh as I checked the time on my phone and said, "You know what,

Annie? We should probably get started. If you wouldn't mind leading the way…"

"Yeah, sure," Annie replied, sounding only slightly confused as she pointed us toward the back of the lobby. "The first floor rooms are this way."

I was sliding my phone back into my pocket when it began to ring. I saw it was Mikey's photo on the screen and motioned for Annie to wait as I put the phone to my ear.

"J-Pop on the chain. Holla at ya boy."

"WHAT?"

"Is this not my Hip-Hop manager?"

Mikey let out an irritated sigh and said, "Lynn told me you two spoke with a girl at the front desk?"

"Yeah, she's…"

Mikey quickly shouted, "IF-SHE'S-RIGHT-THERE-DON'T-SAY-ANYTHING!"

I gestured for Grace and Annie to hold up. "Give me one sec. I gotta take this outside. My new album is about to drop and PR is freakin' about my *Source* cover."

"WHAT?" Grace asked, scowling at me.

"Or you guys can get started without me. Here…" I handed Annie my EMF detector and nodded at Grace. "Why don't you show Annie how to detect ghosts?"

I put the phone to my ear before Grace could object and sprinted to the exit as I said, "Go for J-Pop."

"I need you to subdue the girl."

I had just stepped back out into the sunlight as Mikey said this and at first, I thought I had simply heard him wrong. "Subdue her?"

"Is she still right there?!"

"No, I stepped outside. Grace was pissed. It was hilarious."

"Good boy. Now listen. Lynn saw that this girl had a very unique ring on her left hand. This particular ring means she is a member of a powerful coven and has the potential to be extremely dangerous. I need you to incapacitate her and then put her in the car. Get her out of there ASAP. Grace should have some zip ties in her purse."

"Wait, you're being SERIOUS?"

"I am being very serious. Time is also sort of a factor here."

"Yeah? Well, unfortunately, I'm not a ninja assassin and don't subdue people much, so..."

"Fair point. I'll call Grace." *CLICK.*

I re-entered the lobby just as Grace was answering her phone. "Yeah?"

She listened for a beat and then Grace said, "Sure thing."

She disconnected the call and slid the phone back into her jeans. Annie was using the EMF detector to scan a framed painting of an old ship hanging on the lobby's wall. She was standing with her back to Grace, who abruptly reached an arm around Annie's neck and used her free hand to grip this arm by the wrist, pulling it against Annie's throat and locking her into a chokehold that had the young girl's wide eyes rolling up white in a matter of seconds.

"Holy shit, how is that even POSSIBLE," I said as Annie seemed to pass out almost immediately. Grace sat her on the floor and the softly snoring girl promptly tipped over onto her side. "I thought people only went unconscious like that in movies?"

Grace pointed at her own neck and said, "Baroreceptors in the throat. When they sense a sudden drastic change in blood pressure, they tell the brain to shut off. Like restarting your computer to fix the problem."

Grace tilted her head at me and added, "You don't ever watch MMA?"

"Not really. My family is very Irish, so overly aggressive tatted-up white dudes beating each other bloody isn't that entertaining when it's also how you describe most Thanksgivings."

"That is super interesting," Grace muttered as she retrieved a pair of zip ties from her purse and then rolled the unconscious Annie onto her stomach. "And is it difficult being the only member of your family who ISN'T a real man?"

4

Even though Annie was a thin girl, the dead weight of her unconscious body was enough of a factor that it took both Grace and I to carry her out to the rental car and we managed to get all the way there before realizing neither of us had a hand free to open the trunk.

Grace emitted a frustrated groan as I said, "Well?"

"You're the one with keys, genius."

I rolled my eyes and knelt until I was low enough to gently place Annie's head on the parking lot's gravel covered ground. Grace gave me an exasperated look as I dug the keys from my pocket and she chided, "Wow…could you possibly go any slower?"

"Yeah, sorry. I know my unbridled love for pudding pops can be misleading but transporting unconscious women isn't exactly my specialty!" I shouted, thumbing the rental car's keyless entry and causing the automated trunk to pop open, punctuating my sentence.

I had prepared myself for a lot of possibilities when it came to working for Mikey but knocking out a nice, seemingly innocent girl and stuffing her in a trunk was not one of them. Obviously, I was more than a little irked by the whole situation and Grace's nonchalant attitude was really starting to wear on me.

She scoffed and nodded down at Annie as Grace replied, "Here's a tip. Next time, don't put their head in an ant pile."

"Real cute," I said and then looked down to see that Grace hadn't been joking. "Oh, shit!"

I scrambled to quickly get my hands under Annie just as her eyelids began to flutter and she mumbled, "Ow...what..."

She tried to move her arms but couldn't because of the zip tie binding her wrists together behind her back. Annie's eyes shot open as we quickly lifted her now struggling body into the car's open trunk.

"Are there fucking ants in my hair?!"

"Yeah. Sorry. That was my bad. Don't worry though. We're not gonna like rape you or anything. I promise," I said, trying to sound as sincere as I possibly could while placing a patch of duct tape over her mouth.

I started to use my hand to comb some of the ants from Annie's hair but then Grace shoved me out of the way.

"Watch out," she said as she pulled a small hammer from her purse.

I flinched in unison with Annie as Grace suddenly swung the hammer down inches from the girl's head, hitting it against the inside wall of the trunk.

"What the fuck, Grace?!" I screamed and Annie immediately shouted something against the duct-tape that sounded like, *Yeah, Grace, what the fuck?!*

I leaned forward to see what she had struck: a thin plastic disc attached to a mechanism that was fixed to the trunk's inner wall.

Grace pointed the hammer at the now mangled disc and said, "Safety release for the trunk. In case you accidentally lock yourself inside it. You can't dismantle the release without disabling the trunk's lock all together but you CAN jam the button."

"Something tells me this isn't your first abduction," I said and closed the trunk's lid while trying not to notice how the tape over Annie's mouth inflated with each terrified exhaled.

"Technically, no." Grace tilted her head as she considered something and then she added, "I mean, it's the first time I've ever been the abductor."

"Seriously?"

Grace held out a hand and I gave her the keys as she nodded.

Grace said, "Yeah, I never told you about when I was ten and got kidnapped by Somali pirates?"

"Okay, *suuuure*."

Grace replied with a dismissive gesture as she said, "If you don't believe me, ask Lynn. Or just Google it. I gotta go. Mikey wants me to take her to a motel."

It suddenly dawned on me that Grace had, in fact, been telling the truth just now.

I gestured for her to stop and said, "Wait...is THAT why you're always talking shit about Captain Phillips?"

Grace gave me one of her patented groans as she responded, "All I said was some people don't need freaking Navy SEALS to escape a band of glorified water hobos."

She slid in behind the wheel of the car and shut the door. I started to walk around to the passenger's side when I heard her engage the power locks. I halted in front of the car, pointing down at it and watching through the windshield as Grace started the engine.

"Oh, so I'm staying here? Is that what Mikey said or..."

Grace shifted into reverse and screeched out of the parking spot before throwing the shifter into drive and accelerating away, leaving me standing there pointing down at nothing but the oil-stained gravel and probably looking just as baffled as I felt.

After taking a moment to stare somberly at the cloud of dust Grace had left in her wake, I retrieved the phone from my pocket and started back towards the Beverly. Mikey's number went to voicemail after several rings but by then, I was already back at the entrance to the lobby.

I saw Mikey had returned from the house and was waiting inside with August, who was standing in almost the same spot Annie had been when Grace choked her out a few minutes ago. Mikey was currently examining the EMF detector Annie had dropped and both men turned to look at me as I entered the lobby, their faces contorting into equally quizzical expressions.

I froze in place right there in the doorway, overcome by the sudden and intense feeling that I had just been caught doing something inappropriate.

"How did the sweep go?" Mikey asked.

I figured he was trying to get me to stop acting so weird and play along, so I cleared my throat and said, "Pretty standard. Spikes in the places you'd expect them. No other notable fluctuations, random or otherwise."

"Uh-huh…and where's Grace?"

"She had to go back to the hotel," I replied, pointing a thumb over my shoulder.

Mikey's questioning look became a full-on grimace and I

quickly added, "The OTHER hotel. The one we all stayed at last night."

"Oh. For what?"

"When I asked, she said if she wanted me to know her business then I would and that I was a loser who desperately needed to get his own life before he dies of chronic virginity. I said, 'oh so tampons' and then she punched me in the abdomen and took the keys and now here we are. How was your thing?"

Mikey furrowed his brow at me and replied, "Sort of still doing it."

August gestured at the front desk and said, "Did you see Annie when you came through here last? Pretty girl, short blond hair?"

"Yeah…" I started to say, trying to sound as natural as possible but then my cell began to ring, cutting me off.

I was still holding the phone from when I tried to call Mikey on my walk back from the parking lot and glanced down at the screen to see that the name on the display was his.

"Think you're pocket-dialing me," I said to Mikey as I accepted the call and put the phone to my ear out of simple conditioning. "Hello?"

I had only been expecting to hear the muffled ambiance of Mikey's pants, so you can imagine my surprise when I heard what sounded exactly like his voice saying, "Joel? How'd it go? Were you able to subdue her?"

That familiar nervous feeling suddenly returned, supplemented by an icy dread that began to gnaw at my stomach as the Mikey standing in front of me mouthed the words, *Who is it?*

I pulled the cell from my ear and switched the call to speaker mode as the voice on the phone said, "Hello... Joel?"

"LINUS?!" the real Mikey screamed, suddenly sounding more furious than anyone I've ever heard who was still coherent enough to form actual words.

If Linus' name had been "Kahn," this whole moment would've been bordering on copyright infringement. The voice on the phone, which still sounded exactly like Mikey to me, let out a brief chuckle.

Then he said, "Busted!"

CLICK. Mikey and I exchanged a look that was equal parts confusion and panic. In the several very tense moments of silence that followed, August raised a hand and opened his mouth as if he was going to ask a question but he didn't seem entirely sure as to what that question would be and eventually he just lowered his hand and closed his mouth. Somewhere an elevator chimed and Lynn appeared a moment later.

She saw me and said, "Hey. Where's Grace?"

5

CUT TO:
EXT. THE BEVERLY HOTEL – PARKING LOT – DAY

Mikey shouts…

MIKEY
You what?!

Cue LAUGHTER from the studio audience.

Joel looks uncomfortable. He is sweating profusely. He doesn't feel like himself. He feels somehow detached from reality, like an actor in a show reading lines from a script that will result in a climactic event and everything will eventually work itself out. At least he has that one comfort.

And with it, Joel finds the strength to deliver his next line.
JOEL
YOU were the one who told us to abduct her. Shit, Mikey, that wasn't even the weirdest thing you had me do this week!
Cue more LAUGHTER from the studio audience.

Lynn is there too, pacing. She pulls the phone from her ear and GROANS as she delivers her line.
LYNN
Voicemail again. We gotta try the rental place. See if they can track the car's GPS.

Cue a QUIET MURMURING from the studio audience. Some of them believe that this is all Joel's fault. That he let this happen and if anything bad were to befall Grace as a result, he should be the one held accountable. Some of them have grown more tiny mouths where their eyes should be and they are all screaming at Joel now. Screaming for his flesh as a penance...

———————

"JOEL!"

I managed to snap out of it long enough to realize that Mikey was the one shouting my name.

I blinked and said, "Yeah, sorry...what's up?"

For a brief moment, Mikey's frustrated demeanor slipped away and he gave me a sideways grin.

"Are you high?"

I sighed and said, "I fucking wish."

Mikey seemed to realize something just then and he shot a look at Lynn.

"He got to him, Lynn."

"You don't think..."

I frowned and said, "Who, that Linus dude? I never even met the guy, I swear."

Of course, Mikey completely ignored me and continued, "I think he got to both of them. That's why they were so susceptible to suggestion. Why they thought Linus's voice was mine. LOOK at him. His body is already starting to reject it."

"Reject WHAT?!" I shouted, breaking Grace's rule.

Cue more LAUGHTER from the studio audience.

They are back and now they know something that Joel does not. Something that only intensifies their LAUGHTER to the point where Joel can't even hear Mikey's next line. It sounds like a question.

JOEL

Can you repeat that? I couldn't hear you over all the laughter.

Lynn turns away from Joel and exits frame as she delivers her final line of the scene.

LYNN (O.C.)

Yup, he got to 'em.

Cue another loud bout of LAUGHTER from the studio audience. One of them, a tall green topless woman with AstroTurf dreadlocks for hair and tiny green garden snakes where her nipples should be, nods and mouths the words: Yes, he did.

Mikey grabs Joel by his shoulders and shouts...

MIKEY

Joel!

"...Focus!"

I was suddenly aware of just how shitty I felt, like I'd woken up on the first day of a bad flu. But at least I could hear Mikey again.

He said, "It's vitally important that you try to remember while you're still lucid enough. Do you have any missing time in the past week or so?"

I shook my head and replied, "No…"

"That's what everyone says about missing time. It's difficult to remember the things we can't remember. But REALLY try to think about it. Tell me what you did every day last week."

"Well, I…"

And then it all came rushing back. What followed was a difficult sensation to describe. Have you ever had a necromancer block off memories in your head but he only does a good enough job that it will buy him a few days or so and then all of those memories suddenly return, flooding your mind all at once?

It was like that.

———

Cue the studio audience SPEAKING IN UNISON as Joel begins to lose consciousness and they all jump the railing to rush toward him, bearing their fangs and looking hungry for blood as they scream…

STUDIO AUDIENCE

Dead Things Mikey will return after this brief revelation!

FADE OUT

6

The night I couldn't remember started out normal enough. We had just wrapped up a case the day before and Mikey gave us all the weekend off. Then I got a text at like 8 PM that Saturday from what appeared to be Mikey's number telling me to meet him in half an hour at an address I didn't recognize.

Now, it wasn't exactly unlike Mikey to give us the day off only to call everybody in the moment he got an email that piqued his interest. Though what should have tipped me off was that it was a text. Mikey never texted.

He called and he emailed but texting as a communication option was a concept that he "tolerated at best." Those were Mikey's own words and I should've known something was up, but I didn't because here's the thing: I love my job.

I didn't care that Mikey was calling me in, even if he wasn't technically calling me. Plus, the address was relatively close and in a nice part of town, so I assumed this would end up being more of a social visit. It also wasn't unlike Mikey to call me simply to meet him at some fancy restaurant for lunch because Mauricio's flight home got delayed and he didn't want to eat alone.

The house that I had been summoned to this time was even bigger than Mikey's, though it was located in a more discreet part of the city where property values weren't as high as they were in the Garden District.

Still, it was the kind of place you could refer to as "an estate" without being ironic about it. I pulled into the wide U-shaped driveway and was about to call Mikey to let him know I was there when I got a text from his number saying:

Just park and come to the door.

Now, that last message did seem a little weird to me at the time but you also need to remember that when you work for a guy like Mikey, your tolerance level for "weird" becomes pretty astronomical. I simply assumed he had spotted me pulling up and didn't want my call to interrupt whatever they were doing in there.

So I shrugged and parked the car. I was approaching the front door and just about in knocking range when it was pulled open to reveal an elderly man with a bald head encircled by a fabulous mane of curly silver hair.

"Hello, handsome. You're Mikey's boy, Joel, I presume?" He asked in a tone that was, to put this in politically correct terms: very, very gay.

I nodded at the man and said, "Of course. You can spot me by the content smile and general air of satisfaction regarding my life choices."

"And witty too. I can see why Mikey won't shut up about you. Well, come on in. The gang's out back. I have an issue with my guest house, as it were."

I followed him inside the expansive home and was halted halfway across the living room by a large framed photo of a beautiful woman with vibrant red hair dressed in a sequined form-fitting gown. Basically, she looked like a real-life Jessica Rabbit.

"Got'DAMN. Who's the Firestarter?"

"That's a production still from one of the drag shows I used to put on back in my glory days. That's me," the old man replied, pointing at the picture.

I turned to scowl at him and said, "Shut your lying mouth, you old bald 'mo."

I apologize to anyone offended by the previous statement. Ever since I started working for Mikey, I had been spending a lot of time around gay men and picked up a number of questionable expressions as a result. Of course, the old bald 'mo that I said it too responded by erupting with laughter.

"Tell me about it," he said and let out a somber sigh as he gazed at the photo. "Time makes unjust divas of us all."

"Whoa!" I caught sight of a stack of DVDs on a table beside the framed photo and had scanned the titles out of pure reflex. "You have *Sporloos*? AND *Vampyr*?! Holy shit…"

That's when I saw it, lying there next to the DVDs like it was no big deal.

"You own a boxed copy of *The Flintstones: Surprise at Dinosaur Peak* for the Nintendo Entertainment System?!"

The old man let out a chuckle as he followed me over to the table and said, "All that stuff is my son's, actually."

I gave him a sideways glance and the man nodded. "Yes, my son's. He's about your age."

I picked up the case to feel its weight and sure enough, it felt like a game was in there. I pointed at the box's unsealed lid and said, "May I?"

"Sure," he replied.

I carefully pulled the flap back and slid out the cardboard insert to reveal a pristine cartridge of one of the rarest NES games known to man, rumored to have only been available for rental at Blockbuster Video during the final quarter of 1994.

I scanned the label for signs of a reproduction and saw none. To put this in the clearest terms there are, money: a genuine version of this plastic cartridge of a mediocre game and its corresponding cardboard container were currently worth about five grand.

"Ah, yes. You know what's funny about this particular game?" the old man said, pointing at the cartridge's label.

I glanced over at him, still slightly punch-drunk from the valuable relic I was holding as I replied, "What's that?"

"It's actually an egg," Linus said, his mouth stretching into a dark smile.

I looked back to see that I was now clutching a small white egg. The shell cracked open with a sickening hiss and a dark slimy shape began to emerge from within. I tried to scream and that's when the thing sprung from the egg and into my open mouth, lodging itself in my throat...

7

I awoke to find myself lying on the bed in Mikey's guest room, drenched in sweat and my heart racing. Mauricio was seated beside the bed and patting my forehead with a damp rag.

As my eyelids started to flutter open, I heard him say, "Thank god. Michael?! He's awake."

I started to drift off again and when I opened my eyes next, Mikey was the one standing beside me. I tried to sit up and found that I was too weak to do so.

He said, "Hey there, champ. We're not out of the woods just yet, but you'll be feeling a whole lot better real soon, I promise."

I blinked and he was suddenly holding a clear plastic terrarium with several large roaches skittering about inside it. Mikey set the terrarium down on the bedside table, mere inches from my head. I tried to ask him why but my mouth refused to form the words. I faded out again and when I came to this time, Mikey had warped to the other side of the bedroom.

He was drawing curtains, blotting out the sun until the room's only remaining source of illumination was the tiny bit of light still bleeding in from the hallway. Mikey glanced at me and winked as he crossed the bedroom and abruptly exited, shutting the door behind him and drowning me in utter darkness.

It didn't take long for the feeling to start, a strange pressure along the left side of my head. It wasn't painful, just unnerving. The pressure moved to my ear canal and then, after several extremely uncomfortable moments, it was gone.

I heard something moving along the left side of the bed, the same side that the roach terrarium was on. The movement was accompanied by a faint rhythmic noise that I would soon learn was the sound of a very small person breathing heavily.

The overhead light was switched on to reveal Mikey already halfway across the bedroom, an empty drinking glass in his raised hand. He brought the glass down into the now open terrarium, capturing under it a tiny naked man with partially translucent skin similar to a developing fetus.

He was probably a little thinner and smaller than your pinky (and yes, I AM too classy to make an Asian penis joke here. Also, you should be ashamed of yourself. You know who makes those kinds of jokes? Dudes with little dicks.) I felt a hundred times better than I had just moments ago.

Turning to Mikey, I nodded at the little guy under the glass and said, "What the fuck is THAT?"

"THAT…" Mikey pointed down at the glass and continued, "Is a homunculus."

8

NOTE TO THE FILER: This particular gig clearly got away from us, which is why I labeled it 3-A and the next case 3-B. Also, whichever one of you smelly interns keeps drinking the Code Reds I have stashed in that fridge in the bungalow, consider this your written warning. Mikey told me if I catch someone "red-handed" (Get it? Good. Fuck you!) with my soda, I get to stab said someone twice in a non-vital body part of my choosing.

hugs-n-bitches,

J-Pop

Part 5

CASE FILE #3-B: "Dead Things Mikey and Men of Grosser Blood"

1

Since exposition is lame, we fade in on one of those old-timey black and white educational short films from like the '50s. The kind that kids used to have to watch in school on big loud reel-to-reel projectors.

The film stars Mikey standing beside a bubbling chemistry set while holding a clipboard and wearing a lab coat over a very smart looking sweater vest. He begins by turning to face the camera as he says…

"Hey, kids. It's your old pal, Professor Dead Things Mikey back this time with a really special treat for you. A treat called: Learning!"

The sound of children cheering erupts from off camera and Mikey lifts his free hand, gesturing for the unseen kids to settle down as he continues…

"Okay, class. That's enough. I know. We're ALL super hard right now but let's not get carried away. So, today's subject is the homunculus and we're going to cover your more common questions regarding the topic. What is it? Why is it? Does Kanye West have one? The answers might surprise you."

Mikey holds up three fingers, lowering one as he answers each of the previous questions.

"A tiny man…because somebody splooged in an unfertilized chicken egg while utilizing the lost art of microbioalchemy to produce a miniature copy of themselves…and of course, he does. The little guy is even listed as a co-writer on two different tracks from *808 & Heartbreak*, credited under the pen name T. Sew Eynak."

Mikey turns to give the camera a big smile as he waves goodbye.

"All right, that's all the time we have for today, kids. This has been Professor Dead Things Mikey reminding you to never forget: knowledge IS power. They just don't tell you whose."

2

I exited the attached bathroom to find Mikey still seated beside the bed and leaning forward so that his face was only inches from the terrarium housing Linus' homunculus.

Mikey kept his eyes fixed on the tiny figure under the glass even as he heard me enter and said, "My man...you feeling better?"

"Yeah. A lot...any word on Grace?"

Mikey slowly shook his head.

"Lynn had the rental guy track their GPS but by then the car was already abandoned in a drugstore parking lot. I'm almost certain Linus has them both. So the million-dollar question now is how do we get this bite-sized fuck to tell us his master's master plan."

"Can it do that? Like talk to us?"

Mikey nodded and very confidently said, "It can and it will. The homunculus is more of a photocopy than a clone. It retains all knowledge of the one who spawned it up to the point in which it was first inseminated. Meaning it knows EXACTLY what Linus was thinking when he conceived the little bastard."

I turned to glare at the homunculus, which was nonchalantly munching on the final bit of the roach it had managed to grab before Mikey brought the glass down and without even meaning to, I used my determined Batman voice as I said, "So how do we make it talk?"

Mikey snapped his fingers and replied, "I KNEW the creepy bastards would come in handy eventually."

He then jogged out of the room without further explanation and returned about two minutes later, carrying a red and white ice chest. Mikey bent down to address the homunculus as he said, "Hey there, big guy, you know what a fay spider is?"

Mikey opened the terrarium and dumped in what was currently the prized pig of the disgusting little fay spider entourage he had been housing in his basement since the night he first hired me. The thing immediately began to foam at the mouth and charged the homunculus, shoving the overturned glass containing it against the wall of the terrarium.

The fay spider kept shoving against the drinking glass until it tilted back, its rim lifting slightly and wedging the glass's upturned bottom against the corner of the terrarium's lid. This narrow bit of exposure seemed to give the fay spider a good whiff of the thing under the glass and it liked what it smelled.

The drooling monster went into overdrive, pressing its creepy fang-lined baby's mouth to the floor of the terrarium as it desperately tried to wedge a leg beneath the glass's rim like a dog trying to get at a treat that has slid under the fridge.

The exact words were a bit difficult to decipher over the fay spider's hungry squealing, but what we heard next sounded very similar to a tiny man screaming, "Fuck! Okay! I'll tell you his plan!"

Mikey made a clicking sound with his mouth and said, "*Hässliche…haltepunkt!*"

The fay spider stopped chomping at the overturned glass and spun to face Mikey, who made the clicking sound again as he pointed to the open ice chest on the floor. The fay spider hopped clear over the wall of the terrarium, flying right past my face to land perfectly in the open chest.

Mikey kicked the ice chest closed and pointed at the homunculus as he shouted, "Now start talking or you're going in there with it!"

The little man trapped under the partially tilted glass looked from Mikey to the ice chest and then pointed at both of us as he finally spoke...

3

"Are either of you familiar with the eldritch deity known as Abg'noir? More commonly referred to in text form as: The He Who Waits Below Forbidden Spaces."

The Linus homunculus had a familiar and very pronounced lisp to his voice. One that would have probably required a lesser writer to refer to him as something really un-clever like "homo-culus" but just be thankful that wasn't the case here.

I shook my head and replied, "No."

"Yes," Mikey said and turned to look at me as he clarified. "Abg'noir was initially worshipped by a cultish offshoot of the Kassites around 1500 B.C., instituting a religion that actually thrived for thousands of years after its inception. Fun fact: they were one of the first groups deemed to be 'pagans' by the Catholic church."

Linuculus (which is definitely his name now) pointed at Mikey and said, "That is correct. Abg'noir specializes in rejuvenation of the flesh, making mortal men young again, and also in some cases providing them with eternal life. Master is interested in the third option."

"Yeah...that's what I was afraid of," Mikey replied and then pointed at me. "Remember Beverly's painting of the giant vagina-slug? That's Abg'noir. Well, technically he can appear in a number of ways but that's his true form, which Linus is required to summon to achieve eternal life. That's why he had you two abduct Beverly."

I squinted at Mikey and said, "You mean Annie?"

"My bad. I skipped over that part..."

Mikey twirled one index finger around the other to signal that he was rewinding the explanation as he continued, "If my theory is correct, and it is, then Annie IS Beverly. That painting of Abg'noir in her home? It was an effigy. Apparently, dear sweet Bev was a pretty high-level Wiccan and my guess is when she got sick, she started trying to raise Abg'noir, hoping he would grant her a younger body. Clearly, she succeeded."

Linuculus replied, "That is also correct. Master has been having trouble raising Abg'noir by himself."

Mikey balled his hands into fists as he turned to glare at the homunculus and said, "It was him causing the paranormal activity at the hotel, wasn't it? All so he could get me called over there by an unassuming third party and bait my employees into abducting his mark for him, that shiny-headed son of a whore..."

I was still in shock from the whole Beverly-Annie revelation and before Linuculus could answer, I interjected to say, "Okay, hold up. You just blew my mind like this was spring break and it had cocaine. I need a second to review here."

Linuculus shook his head at me and, in a foreboding tone, he said, "You do not have many seconds to spare if you wish to save your friend and the innkeeper's wife. I do not know exactly where Master plans to conduct the ritual but I do know that if he manages to raise Abg'noir's true form, those you care for will be consumed in sacrifice."

Mikey jabbed a thumb at Linuculus and said, "The little fuck is right. We gotta move."

"I agree but where? Where around here can Linus even

conduct a ritual to raise Abby-Gwar's true form? I mean, I'm hardly an expert on the matter but that's gotta be a short list of places, right?"

Mikey thumbed the screen on his phone and then put it to his ear as he said, "Actually, that is right. And I'm pretty sure I know exactly which place he's going to pick."

4

Mikey first met Linus when the former was only 25 and the latter was 53. The older man had been standing in a drugstore parking lot at 3 AM on a Wednesday. It had been the tail end of Linus's professional drag days, which landed him in New Orleans the previous fall.

Currently, Linus was putting on three shows a week at the Love Lost Lounge for what was at the time a very vibrant drag scene. And even at 53, he was still able to play up that Jessica Rabbit bit well enough to pull in the bi-curious tourist market which was a sought-after demo in the local gay bar economy.

Though that night it wasn't Linus's drag alter ego, Miss Labia Plath, that Mikey spotted as he first pulled into the mostly vacant parking lot but rather "merely lil' ole Linus" standing there beside his empty Chevy Nova, talking to no one.

At least, that's what it had looked like to Mikey. Feeling compelled to solve the mystery before him, he found a parking space that was close enough to hear what the weirdo was saying. Mikey sat there in his car and watched as the older gentleman across from him reached a hand into his Nova's open passenger window and said…

"See? I told you I wasn't going to be long and you were all like, 'Nuh-uh! Don't leave me! You're gonna be forever!' But I wasn't. I was very fast."

Just as Mikey was assuring himself that this nut job was

actually holding a conversation with an imaginary friend, he saw the head of a very adorable Australian Shepherd appear at the Nova's open window, looking to be rewarded with a thorough petting for having waited so patiently. Linus had been talking to his dog. Right then and there was when Mikey fell in love with him.

That night, Linus was approached and subsequently knocked head over heels by this ruggedly attractive twenty-something asking him about Rosa Barks, and of course, he was all too willing to claim that he loved Mikey back. And he probably had, in his own way at some point in the ten years they spent together.

Both would go on to deprive the other of vital secrets, sure, but certainly not affection. In that time, it seemed like there were more than enough lust-inspired platitudes to keep the two of them going until the sun went supernova. Though of course, like all truly perfect things, it could not last.

Linus was born a natural empath and had grown to be a novice necromancer by the time he and Mikey met. At that point, Mikey had just returned from a year-long pilgrimage to India, which he spent learning under the tutelage of a world-renowned Shaman. Mikey and Linus quickly discovered that, despite the age difference between them, they had a lot of overlapping interests.

The problem was, though, as much as Linus might've cared for Mikey, he cared for cocaine that much more. Before they met, Linus had been practicing the dark arts as a hobby, something to keep him busy between drag shows. But selling coke to support his habit was Linus's primary profession.

It was actually Mikey who first showed Linus how to harness his true potential as a necromancer, though he reiterated to me that Mikey had no way of knowing Linus would go on to use that ability to con mourning families into thinking they were being stalked by their recently deceased loved ones. I guess that was Mikey's first red flag that their relationship was headed for rocky shores.

Then Linus' supplier went dry and everything changed. By that point, he was so sure of his skills as a necromancer that Linus decided to go straight to his dealer's source overseas to find out what the problem was and to offer his services in fixing said problem. What happened after that involved amassing rebel forces, a lot of needless bloodshed, and the eventual overthrow of a sadistic warlord.

For Mikey, it was another one of those dark times in his life that he really didn't like talking about, which was understandable. I didn't really like hearing about it. Especially the part where Mikey had to stop the car and pull over because he was crying too hard to drive. That was super awkward.

And I really don't want to advocate raising the dead as a solution to anyone's problems but for what it's worth, necromancers are apparently a perfect hard counter to warlords. See, because warlords pop up fast and leave a lot of dead bodies lying around nearby, just waiting for any jackoff in a black robe who knows a bit of backward Latin to come and raise them into his own personal undead army. Apparently, that was all Linus had to do to get his coke supply back.

I'm probably simplifying the whole ordeal a bit more than it deserves to be but we were pressed for time when Mikey told me this story and he wasn't able to elaborate on many of the details. All he said was that once Linus took out the local warlord, he became quite tight with "El Capitán" of the drug smuggling operation he'd gone there to restore. After that, Linus started transporting massive quantities of cocaine into the U.S.

The ungodly amount of money he was now making as a result didn't mean Linus was going to stop conning grieving families into forking over their life savings, though; quite the contrary. Linus's deep pockets and renewed confidence in his abilities allowed him to take his necromancy hustle to an entirely new level. And just to reiterate, Linus did all this while also secretly trafficking large quantities of cocaine into the United States on a monthly basis.

Of course this story has a very unhappy ending, but not the one you're probably thinking of. Linus actually never got busted by the feds or anything like that. He had simply been so wrapped up in "business" that by the time Linus was finally notified that his son from a previous marriage had been diagnosed with a rare and extremely fatal blood disease, it was already too late.

Linus was actually "working a case" at the time and had long since stopped taking his ex-wife's calls. She actually had to track down Mikey's number and tell him and when word finally did reach Linus, he didn't even have enough time to tell the boy goodbye.

After his son's death, Linus became determined to use his powers to bring the boy back. This was a mistake, as Mikey tried to warn him it would be, but by that point, Linus was so blinded by the guilt of not being there for his dying child that he could no longer see his choices clearly. If he could've, he would've seen that the biggest problem with his plan was also the most obvious.

In over a decade of practicing necromancy, Linus had never managed to just once "bring someone back all the way," which meant complete with a fully functioning brain and organs and NOT as some saggy-skinned r-tard who couldn't even walk straight like the kind that Linus was used to raising. Remember Janet from Case File #0?

The only reason she seemed so coherent at the time was because Linus had stuck a homunculus in her, as well (apparently, they were a big part of his hustle.) In Linus's defense, though, bringing someone back all the way was something that even the world's most skilled necromancers had difficulty doing with any consistency.

Plus, Linus didn't have much practice in trying to since in the past, resurrecting corpses with a fully functioning brain would've been counterintuitive to his hustle. Of course, this time it was his son that Linus was bringing back and nothing less than "all the way" would do.

But really, how difficult could it be to do something that only the best in your field can pull off and that you personally had never even attempted to do before that night? (Spoiler alert: really fucking difficult.)

Despite all of that, Linus went through with the ritual to resurrect his son anyway and just the sight of the thing that began shambling towards him in the end was enough for him to know that he had failed.

That night, Mikey had to sit there and watch as the man he loved beat the son he couldn't save to death with the same shovel they had used to unearth his grave. Of course, that sort of thing tends to fundamentally change a person. How had August said Beverly put it? "Like losing a vital part of your humanity."

Linus was a different person after that night. He became a brooding hurtful stranger who even had the gall to blame the outcome of his undead son's resurrection on Mikey, claiming it was his fault for so adamantly trying to talk Linus out of it beforehand and depriving him of the confidence required to bring his son back properly.

That's when things started to get really bad. Linus grew beyond hurtful into full-on abusive, giving Mikey no other choice but to leave him. Linus resented Mikey for dissolving their decade-long relationship at such a dark point in his own life, which Linus saw as Mikey abandoning him in his hour of need. As it turned out (and you might've already guessed this), Linus could be a real vengeful prick when he felt so inclined.

This was one of those times. It didn't help that Mikey began ratting on his ex to numerous "former clients" (which was what Linus had called the families involved in his necromancy cons) in a desperate bid to alleviate some of the mountain of guilt he had accumulated while dating Linus. Word of his ex's nefarious deeds got around and Linus was forced into hiding, only to emerge more than ten years later with what seemed to be a raging hate-on for Mikey.

The fact that Linus's former lover had spent the time he was away building a successful reputation as a legitimate and effective paranormal freelancer to the rich and powerful was apparently something that Linus saw as a direct slight to his own illegitimate racket.

Linus didn't see Mikey's legitimacy as anything but a snub,

an attempt to further one-up his own success. Because that is the way crazy people think and Linus was really fucking crazy. Not sure if I have to explain that at this point, but just in case anyone missed it...

The guy who put a little man in my head because my boss broke up with him sometime during the release of the *Star Wars* prequels is really fucking crazy.

5

As a result of their prior relationship, Mikey knew Linus' favorite spot in the city to conduct summonings. It was the same location he had chosen to resurrect his son.

A small isolated patch of woods in City Park positioned somewhere between the public golf course and Tad Gormley Stadium. There was a narrow clearing hidden at the center of these woods and on this clearing many years ago someone had constructed a twenty-foot tall wooden platform for reasons that have since been lost to time.

The platform wasn't situated high enough to see over the trees (though I guess it could've been at one point) and the only view it provided was a slightly elevated version of the one you already had. The clearing itself wasn't very big in relation either, roughly thirty feet across with the platform taking up a majority of the available real estate, leaving a little under ten feet of open ground between its foundation and the surrounding woods.

According to Mikey, most summoning rituals required a natural setting that was located somewhere isolated with an unobstructed view of the sky. Just as I had correctly assumed, there was maybe a handful of spots in all of New Orleans that met these criteria and the City Park clearing was the only one with the added convenience of having its own platform.

What made Mikey so absolutely sure that Linus would pick the clearing this time was that the ritual for summoning

Abg'noir required "a regurgitation of small divine slug-like beings that consume the soil beneath the effigy of the He Who Waits provided by the ritual's conductor, transforming the very ground into a doorway through which the true form of Abg'noir may pass."

Mikey finished reading aloud from the wiki page on Abg'noir and looked up at me as he added, "I don't know about you but that sounds like the kind of summoning where I'd want an elevated platform to stand on."

Mikey had asked Lynn to meet us on the first green of the City Park Golf Course where we found her waiting thirty minutes later. It was dusk by then and Lynn was at the edge of the green, seated beside the canister of gasoline Mikey had told her to bring and using a small flashlight to read a book amidst the fading daylight.

Mikey nudged me with an elbow and nodded at Lynne as he said, "We're about to potentially face off against an eldritch god and this cold-blooded gangster is so relaxed about the whole ordeal that she's sitting here, reading...what?"

Lynn greeted us with a guilty smile as she quickly flashed the cover of the paperback in her hands and said, "Um, one of the *True Blood* books?"

Mikey slowly shook his head as he replied, "And thusly, the illusion was shattered...how is it?"

"Honestly? My niece gave them to me and I assumed I was gonna hate 'em but they're actually really good."

"REALLY?"

Lynn nodded and I did my best Bill Compton impression as I added, "I am vampire, Sookie."

Mikey slowly glanced at both of us as he said, "Anyway...we

should really get going. Joel, I'll grab the gasoline. Can you take this?"

Mikey was referring to the Duffle bag he had carried from his car which contained several weights from a barbell set as well as a bundle of climbing rope and a small fire extinguisher. I nodded and tried not to grunt too loudly from the strain of taking the bag as I draped the strap over my shoulder.

"There was definitely a bit of movement in those woods since I've been here," Lynn said as she marked her place and stashed the novel behind the tree she had been leaning against. "All of it human, though, from what I could tell. Two, maybe three hired hands."

"Then we'll walk softly," Mikey replied and bent to retrieve the gas canister as Lynn stood and slid a Colt Model 1911 handgun with a .50 caliber conversion kit on it from a holster on her hip.

"Good, because I'm carrying a big stick tonight," Lynn said and pulled back the slide, chambering a round as she nodded. "All right, boss...lead the way."

She then turned and promptly walked off into the darkening wilderness, holding the gun so that it pointed upward at a safe angle and with her trigger finger pressed flat against the space beneath the slide. She looked like a tiny bespectacled Rambo stalking off into the woods.

When Mikey started heading into those same woods but in a different direction, I pointed and said, "Wait. Shouldn't we be following the reservoir dog?"

"She'll make her way back around to us. Lynn knows what she's doing. Don't worry. I've got a gun, too. See?"

Mikey retrieved the little .32 caliber revolver he had in a

shoulder holster hidden under his blazer. He passed the gun to his other hand so that the butt of it was pointing towards me when he held it out.

"Would you feel better if you were the one holding it?"

I took the gun and examined it as I followed Mikey into the woods while muttering, "But hers was a lot bigger."

Mikey replied with a scoff. "Story of my life."

"Ha!" I said with a brief chuckle. "I get that one now."

6

With that heavy-as-shit Duffle bag draped over me, it was difficult to move as smoothly as Lynn had been, but I still held the gun pointed up like I'd seen her doing and put on my game face as we made our way through the woods, my eyes darting back and forth across the darkening spaces between the trees that surrounded us and straining to listen for approaching footsteps over Mikey's incessant ranting. And he really was earning that adjective, too.

Mikey was currently answering a question that no one had asked as he said, "The moon will be out soon and assuming Linus had Beverly make him a new effigy, that's the only thing he needs to begin the sacrifice. Moonlight is crucial to most summonings. A full moon works the best, obviously. A harvest moon, now THAT'S what you really want but any full moon will still give you beneficial results. Looks like tonight it's a...waxing gibbous."

"Tell me about it," I replied in a tone that an ex-girlfriend once dubbed "severely sarcastic."

I stopped actually listening to Mikey once I realized that he was babbling on like this as a way of drawing out any potential assholes Linus had patrolling the stretch of woods we were currently moving through. And sure enough, it didn't take long to prove effective.

A twig snapped somewhere behind the trees to my left and I dropped the duffle bag as I crouched and slowly started to back up, raising the revolver I was clutching in both hands and aiming it at the two men that had been stalking toward us.

They spotted Mikey, who continued walking forward while acting oblivious to my actions, but the men hadn't noticed me yet. They were both carrying pump action shotguns and there wasn't a shirtsleeve between them.

Now, this is the part in most action movies where the good guy shouts something like "Freeze!" or "Don't even think about it, dirtbag!" because he is a cop or whatever and has some form of actual authority. I did not and I also had never shot anybody before. As fun as it looked in GTA, I found that in for-real life it wasn't exactly an easy thing to bring myself to do.

Lucky for me, though, just as one of the men began to raise his weapon toward Mikey, a familiar Colt 1911 emerged from the tree beside him as its barrel was pressed snuggly against his groin. The man froze while in the process of aiming his shotgun at Mikey.

The other guy gave his buddy a confused look and muttered, "What are you doin'? He's gettin' away."

The first man used his eyes to direct his friend's attention to the large handgun currently nuzzling his dick as he replied, "Uh…we might have a problem."

"Damn right you do," Lynn said, still hidden behind the tree. "Joel, you got a bead on the other one?"

I aimed the revolver at the guy without Lynn's gun in his lap and shouted, "Yup!"

Both men looked surprised to see me standing there and I nodded a hello, winking at them. Lynn took the first guy's shotgun as she stepped out from behind the tree and passed it back to Mikey when he approached a moment later.

Mikey aimed the shotgun at the other man and said, "All right, sweetheart...you wanna be all Chuck Heston about this or can we do it the easy way where you hand that thing over like a gentleman and everybody gets to keep their genitals?"

The man considered Mikey's words as he glanced down at the gun Lynn was still pressing to his cohort's junk. After a very tense beat, he handed his weapon to Lynn and then immediately turned to sprint off into the woods.

"That asshole," the first guy said as he turned to watch his buddy go. "He was my damn ride."

The man ran off to follow his friend into the darkness as Mikey laughed. I let out an exhale, not realizing how tensely I had been holding my weapon until I finally lowered it and felt the ache in my forearms.

"Where does he find these morons?" Mikey asked as he unloaded the shotgun he was holding and pocketed the shells before tossing the gun into a nearby bush.

Lynn did the same with the other guy's gun as she slowly scanned the surrounding woods, an uneasy expression on her face.

Lynn said, "I don't know but there still might be more wandering around, so let's not get sloppy now."

"How long have you known me, Lynn? When do I ever do anything sloppy?" Mikey asked and then turned, pointing down the narrow path we had been following. "Besides, the clearing is right up there."

Lynn looked where he was pointing and replied, "Where?"

"My guess is past those trees where that flashing light is

coming from," I said and as if on cue, there was another flash of light.

"Well, shit. That was fast," Mikey muttered.

He started jogging toward the light as Lynn chased after him. I snatched up the heavy duffle bag and slung it over my shoulder, hurrying to meet up with them just as Lynn and Mikey reached the edge of the clearing.

We emerged right in front of the platform but close enough that we couldn't be seen by anyone actually standing on it unless they were to lean over the railing running along its edge and look directly down, which is exactly what Grace was doing when we exited the woods.

I almost screamed her name when I spotted her kneeling beneath the railing with her face pointed down at the ground but then I saw Grace's expression, which was a combination of equal parts terror and agony. I understood the first part but not the second until she started to heave forward and I remembered that word from the Wiki entry on Abg'noir: regurgitation.

Grace's mouth flew open to emit a brief spray of black slime and then a slug-like creature about the size of a small legless Doxin began to inch its way up from her throat. After several painful-sounding moments of intense gagging, the slug-thing slid free of her mouth and then dropped down into a pit in the ground located a few yards ahead of us.

This pit appeared to be the source of the flashing light we had seen. It was radiating the same strange pink glow and there was another flash as the slug plummeted into it, revealing for a brief moment the dense mass of writhing slug-things lining the inside wall of the immense hole. I looked back up just as Grace began to heave again.

I felt someone squeezing my arm and turned to see Mikey holding up the canister of gasoline as he said, "I need Lynn to watch my back while I clear out the portal. Remember the plan. Wait for Linus to spot us and his attention to be diverted. Then get him to stop chanting."

The chanting he was referring to was currently emanating from the platform above us and the words being repeated were from some long-dead tongue that I didn't recognize, but to me, it sounded like Linus was saying, *"Yogurt un-fun all blobby star frog Abby Gwar!"*

There was so much to take in when we first reached the clearing that I hadn't actually noticed the chanting until Mikey pointed it out but once he did, it was like Linus was suddenly standing right beside me as he recited the words, which forced their way into my mind and abruptly derailed my train of thought until the chanting was all I could hear...

"Yogurt un-fun all blobby star frog Abby Gwar! Yogurt un-fun all blobby star frog Abby Gwar!"

I fought off a sudden wave of nausea and shut my eyes as I struggled to clear my head. Mikey moved his hand from my arm to my shoulder as I heard him say from what sounded like very far off...

"Sing the *Sanford and Son* theme song."

"What?"

"Do you know it?"

"Yeah..."

"It's a scientific fact that if you have a song stuck in your head, singing the melody from the *Sanford and Son* theme will get it out."

With my eyes still shut and an arm clutching my stomach, I did as Mikey suggested:

"Bad-uh-bad-ump...bad-uh-bad-ump-bad-uh-bad-ump-bad-uh-bad-ump..."

The worst of the nausea had passed by then and I slowly nodded to signal that it was working.

Eventually, I opened my eyes to face Mikey and said, "You never told me how I was supposed to stop Linus once I get up there."

"Well, Joel, let's see. He put a homunculus in your head. Just tonight, he paid men to hunt us with shotguns and he's currently about to feed Grace to a giant slug-vagina to get back at me for dumping him, so..." Mikey pointed down at the gun in my hand and said, "My vote is for as painfully as possible."

7

I made my way around to the back of the tall wooden structure and left the Duffle bag at the base of the narrow stairs leading up to the platform so that I could climb them as quietly as possible. I had Mikey's gun raised and his parting words to me running through my head on a loop as I mounted each creaking wooden step.

And most of my former Lit professors might be disappointed to hear that, despite all of the many volumes of renowned prose I've been forced to consume over the years, the one quote that came to me in that particular moment of existential crisis was a Cypress Hill lyric:

Here is something you can't understand...how I can just kill a man!

I reached the top of the platform right as another slug-thing was sliding from Grace's open mouth and she let out an involuntary sob that made Linus pause his chanting to emit a quick chuckle. And that was all it took.

Suddenly, I didn't care about waiting for his attention to be diverted or the sanctity of human life. Sure, there was no telling what it meant against the vast ripples of time and space to snuff out the light of another but right then and there, I was coming up short on fucks to give about space's ripples.

I started over to Linus with my fingers tight around the handle of the gun and it was Annie who saw me first. I hadn't noticed her standing there beside Linus and chanting along with him, her wrists bound together by a length of padlocked chain that was secured to the platform's railing. She hadn't noticed me either until I started forward with a gun in my outstretched hands.

Annie's eyes went wide as she suddenly stopped chanting to let out a gasp. She tried to play it off by pretending to have fumbled the words as she resumed chanting but by that point, it was already too late.

"What?" Linus asked as he briefly paused his own chanting again to turn and glance at her.

I rushed forward, taking this opportunity to clear the rest of the space between myself and them. Linus quickly turned back when he heard my hurried footsteps to find the barrel of Mikey's .38 sticking into the side of his face.

"Annie, be a dear. Stop chanting," I said and Annie nodded, closing her mouth.

Linus scoffed as he started to say something and that's when I shot his jaw off his face. Seriously, like clean off. Of course, that hadn't been my plan or anything and it looked fucking ridiculous. Like when Daffy Duck takes a point blank shotgun blast and he has to turn his beak back around to the front of his head.

At that range, the round from the little .32 pierced straight through one jaw hinge and then clear out the other, taking with it the whole bottom of Linus's face as he then turned to glare at me with his tongue dangling from his bald head in the brief moment before the old man finally toppled over.

I hurried to kneel beside a dazed-looking Grace, who had stopped heaving once the chanting ceased. I saw that her wrists were chained together as well.

"The key's in his pocket!" Annie shouted to me as she knelt to retrieve it from Linus's still convulsing body.

She unlocked herself and then hurried over to us as I placed a hand on Grace's back and tried to get her to look at me.

"Grace, you okay?"

"Here you go," Annie said, handing me the key as she stared at Grace with an expression of abject pity.

I started to unlock her wrists as I glanced up at Annie and said, "I'm real sorry about that whole abduction thing. I had a little man in my head making me do stuff. It's a long story. Anyway, can I ask you for a favor? There's a Duffle bag at the bottom of the stairs over there..."

Annie rolled her eyes and started toward the stairs as I shouted, "Thanks!"

I heard a faint scoff and turned to see the slightest hint of a smile starting at the edges of Grace's mouth as she muttered, "You are such a dick."

"What? HOW does that make me a dick?!"

"Getting a girl to carry a heavy bag up a flight of stairs for you?"

"If anything, that makes me a feminist."

She was now full on smirking as Grace replied, "Oh, BOOOOOO..."

"I was staying up here to comfort you!" I shouted over her in an indignant tone.

Grace scoffed and rolled her eyes as she said, "Yeah? Stellar plan. I can tell you came up with it."

I heard grunting behind us and looked back to see Annie dragging the Duffle bag up the last few steps. I stood and thanked her again. I was about to start across the platform to carry the bag the rest of the way but then Mikey shouted…

"Joel, can we get an update here?!"

"I'm fine! Everybody's fine! Linus is dead, I think!" I shouted back as I turned to look down. "I shot his HOLY SHIT!"

I looked down at the pit below for the first time and what I saw was a shimmering whirlpool of slug-things roughly ten feet deep and centered around a plaster statue that was basically a much smaller more simplistic version of the Abg'noir installation we had seen in August's living room. The statue was at the bottom of the pit, being slowly consumed by something that vaguely resembled a spinning ball of pink DayGlo paint.

Mikey flipped open a Zippo lighter and ignited it as Lynn finished pouring out the canister of gasoline onto the churning mass of slug-things. He dropped the lit Zippo into the pit and the entire slug whirlpool was engulfed in flames, everything except for the ball of DayGlo paint at the bottom and the partially consumed effigy which appeared to be completely unaffected by the fire.

Mikey turned his attention back to me as he said, "Looks like we're already too far along down here. I'm gonna have to pull the effigy out manually. Can you ready the rope?"

I gave Mikey a thumbs up and turned to find that Grace had taken the Duffle bag from Annie and was now aiming a raised middle finger my way as she lugged it over to the edge of the platform.

"I just shot a man who was making you vomit giant slugs. Not asking for a thank you here. But as a sign of gratitude, maybe you could refrain from making obscene gestures at me," I said as I motioned to the small puddle of blood where Linus's jawless body had been.

And then I realized the problem with the preceding description and added, "Um, ladies? Where's Linus?"

8

Even the remains of his dismembered jaw were missing.

Annie pointed a thumb back at the stairs as she said, "He didn't pass me on the way down, I can tell you that."

"Joel?" Mikey shouted in a tone bordering on annoyance. "Time is sort of a factor here!"

I turned back to look down at Mikey as I replied, "So, minor issue. We lost Linus's body."

"Yeah, he does that. We'll worry about him when we can. Right now, we've got bigger fish. Or, you know, slugs," Mikey said and gestured down at the pit.

By now, the effigy was more than halfway consumed by the dayglow ball and the fire had reduced the surrounding whirlpool of slugs to a charred mess. Grace retrieved the fire extinguisher from the duffle bag and dropped it down to Lynn as I wrapped the nylon climbing rope around the railing a couple of times and then tossed one end of it down to Mikey.

I secured weights to the other end and stood on them as I braced myself against the railing and wrapped the rope around my arm, giving it a tug to signal that I was in place. Lynn had used the extinguisher to put out most of the bigger flames and Mikey gave the pit a cursory scan to ensure that none of the slugs were still moving around. Then he turned his back to the pit and repelled down into it.

Grace was standing beside me and helped slowly feed the line out to Mikey as he descended the wall of charred slug-things below. Just as he reached the effigy and started to tug it loose, the pink dayglow ball began to expand into a flat disc.

That disc became a sort of warped window, like a giant fisheye lens looking out across the red sands of a vast desert landscape. In the distance was a floating diamond-shaped structure that appeared to be the throne of a massive slug-like being with a pulsating vulva on its slimy underside. For a brief moment, we forgot ourselves.

And by that I mean, we all literally forgot that we were individual sentient beings here on planet Earth in the human year 2016 and for one very brief wink in time all that we knew was Abg'noir, the He Who Waits Below Forbidden Spaces and Knows the Many Names of Darkness for He Consumes the Souls of All Forsaken Children So That the Abyss May One Day Sing Her Song to Him As Well...

And then Mikey was looking up at us as he yanked the effigy loose and screamed, "NOW!"

Grace and I quickly ducked beneath the railing, pulling the weights along with us and letting them drop off the side of the platform as I wrapped the rope around my other arm and Grace wrapped her arms around me. We were yanked down over the side by the falling weights and both of us just barely managed to land standing on the tiny round platform they provided.

Mikey was hoisted up by the pulley effect this had on his end of the rope but not by much and we looked down into the pit to see that a large cluster of hideous globular faces with mouths full of long pointy translucent teeth like that of an Angler fish had emerged from the orifice on Abg'noir's underside. The nearest face was sticking out from the portal with its foaming mouth clamped around Mikey's left ankle.

Oh, my god…what do we do?!

That had been my first thought while we hung there helplessly above the pit but before I could even start to properly process it, the wall of charred slug-things in front of Mikey began to stir as one of them suddenly lunged out from beneath the others and clamped itself onto Mikey's right eye.

What do we do?! WHAT DO WE DO?!

Mikey began to scream and I felt someone grabbing onto my ankles. It was Lynn. She was lifting up her legs and straining to hold on to me as she attempted to use her own weight to pull us farther down, which she managed to do by a whole five inches.

Below us, Mikey's screaming intensified until finally he swung his arm forward and chucked the effigy up to the edge of the pit, where it danced along the rim for one obnoxiously long moment before finally rolling out onto the surrounding grass.

The portal beneath Mikey shrunk to a tiny radiant point of pink light, leaving behind the severed face of the thing that had bit down onto Mikey's foot (I later found out that cluster of faces had been Abg'noir's genitals. Apparently, eldritch gods have genitals. The more you know, right?)

Mikey shot up out of the pit and Lynn released my ankles, rolling out of the way just as Grace and I plummeted to the ground. She hurried over to Mikey as he limped toward us on his mangled foot, gritting his teeth. Mikey used both hands to grab onto the slug-thing still covering his right eye and Lynn gasped.

"Mikey, wait…"

He yanked on the slug-thing, dislodging it as he dropped to his knees and emitted a painful moan that was so loud, I had to cover my ears and turn away. But not before I got an accidental glimpse of the mangled eye socket below that slug.

Even with my complete lack of medical expertise, I was pretty confident there was nothing salvageable there. It was like looking down into an open can of Hunt's Manwich. Coincidentally, if the people in charge of marketing over at Hunt's see this? You're welcome.

9

Lynn handed over the keys to Mikey's Porsche and asked me to drive Annie back to the Beverly so she and Grace could ride with Mikey to the hospital. Those were Lynn's only instructions but on the drive there, Annie and I got to talking and I discovered that she had wanted desperately to tell her husband who she really was this whole time but was terrified that August wouldn't believe her.

So, when we arrived at the Beverly at a little after midnight, I felt obliged to walk the young (well seemingly young) girl inside and August was right there, waiting for us at the entrance to the lobby. He yanked open the door, looking beyond worried, and very politely demanded an explanation.

I volunteered to have a sit down with them and helped Annie explain the whole story. I had worked with Mikey long enough by now that I was familiar with most of the specific terminologies and syntax he would've used to describe a case like this. So I attempted to do the same, reciting Mikey's terms and his fun facts as if they were my own so naturally that I was secretly sort of freaking myself out.

In the end, August was so satisfied with our explanation and of course elated to discover that his deceased wife had returned to him as an attractive 19-year-old girl that he actually shook my hand as I was leaving. And this was AFTER I had told him about cramming his wife into the trunk of a car.

I called Grace as soon as I was back on the road but there

was no answer from her or Lynn for most of the drive home. Finally, just as I reached city limits, my phone rang. It was Grace, calling to tell me they had moved Mikey out of ICU and he was doing a lot better.

Mikey really wanted to talk to Mauricio but he wasn't answering his cell. He was probably just asleep because it was like 5 AM at this point. So, would I mind swinging by Mikey's house to wake him up and let him know what was going on?

I hadn't noticed that Mikey's front door was sitting open until I was out of the Porsche and halfway up the driveway. A familiar sensation suddenly returned to me, a sickening premonition that something was extremely off here. Mikey's door being ajar wasn't something that happened on accident. The trail of blood in the foyer confirmed it.

As he heard me begin to approach the living room, Linus shouted, "That's right, you stupid little whore! This whole night has been one big distraction! Something to keep you busy while I took from you the thing you cared about the most in this world! Let's see how YOU like it!"

Something about his voice wasn't quite right. I learned the cause as I entered the living room to see Linus seated on the floor, his disfigured jaw having been reattached with what looked like fishing line. The flesh of it had darkened at the edges and was turning a sickly yellow hue.

Linus was clutching Mauricio's lifeless wide-eyed body in the crook of his arm and using his free hand to cut a thin slit along the side of the dead man's face. Though he abruptly stopped once he saw that it was me entering the room.

Linus sounded almost annoyed as he muttered, "Well, this is embarrassing..."

About the Author

Joel was born, raised, and still resides in the city of New Orleans. When he isn't writing creepy-ass novels, Joel can be found scripting subversive internet comedy for the likes of such shows as the award-winning web-series, "Agents of Cracked." He spends way too much time playing video games, and his best friend is a 7-year-old autistic Border Collie named Agro. When Joel grows up, he wants to be a Space Cowboy. You can follow him on Twitter @Joel_C_Farrelly if you're into that.

Thought Catalog, it's a website.
www.thoughtcatalog.com

Social
facebook.com/thoughtcatalog
twitter.com/thoughtcatalog
tumblr.com/thoughtcatalog
instagram.com/thoughtcatalog

Corporate
www.thought.is

Made in the USA
Middletown, DE
06 April 2021